Whatever you like to read,
Red Fox has got the story for you.
Why not choose another book from our range of
Animal Stories, Funny Stories or Fantastic Stories?
Reading has never been so much fun!

RED FOX ANIMAL STORIES

OMELETTE: A CHICKEN IN PERIL

Gareth Owen,
illustrated by Katinka Kew

RED FOX FUNNY STORIES

THANKS FOR THE SARDINE

Written and illustrated
by Laura Beaumont

GIZZMO LEWIS: FAIRLY SECRET AGENT

Michael Coleman

RED FOX FANTASTIC STORIES

THE STEALING OF QUEEN VICTORIA

Shirley Isherwood,
illustrated by George Buchanan

THE INFLATABLE SHOP

Willis Hall, illustrated by Babette Cole

Fowl Pest

James Andrew Hall

Illustrated by Lucy Case

RED FOX

A Red Fox Book

Published by Random House Children's Books
20 Vauxhall Bridge Road, London SW1V 2SA

A division of Random House UK Ltd
London Melbourne Sydney Auckland
Johannesburg and agencies throughout the world

1 3 5 7 9 10 8 6 4 2

First published in Great Britain by
The Bodley Head Children's Books 1994

Published in paperback by Red Fox 1994

This Red Fox edition 1999

Printed in Norway by AIT Trondheim AS

RANDOM HOUSE UK Limited Reg. No. 954009

ISBN 0 09 940182 7

Author's Note

It is almost impossible to be one hundred per cent accurate in translating Chicken into English. As Professor H.E.N. Coope has pointed out, in his well-known poultry primer *Chick Speak*, the meaning of a phrase can be totally altered by the style of delivery. A quick 'Waarrk Quaarrk', for example, means 'Lay off' whereas a more leisurely 'Waaarrrk Quaaarrrk' means 'Pleased to meet you'. I am grateful to Professor Coope, the leading authority in the field of farmyard phonetic languages, for allowing me to make liberal use of his manual and of his time during the writing of this book.

Dedicated to
THE VERY LAST BATTERY HEN

Chapter One

When she was eight, Amy Pickett wanted to be a chicken.

'My mother was,' she said.

'Your mother rides a bicycle,' said Clarice Cooper. 'Since when did hens ride bikes?'

They were walking to school.

'*That* lady is called Mrs Pickett,' said Amy. 'She only adopted me.'

'You're cracked,' said Clarice.

They almost always went to school together. If the weather was really horrible, Mr Pickett drove them in his van.

'You don't look anything like a chicken,' said Clarice. 'You haven't got a beak. Or claws. Where are your feathers?'

1

'On the bits you can't see,' said Amy.

And she made off down the lane, squawking and flapping her elbows.

The Picketts and the Coopers lived next door to each other, at the very edge of the village. Amy and Clarice were best friends, though nobody could explain why. To tell the truth (and that was something Amy found quite difficult to do) they were as opposite as water is from fire.

Sensible Clarice was black. She wore glasses. She could play chess and a recorder. She could even speak French. Amy, on the other hand, had wicked red hair and quaint habits. *Her* recorder lay in three pieces in a cupboard under the stairs. And she was far too flighty to concentrate on anything as deep as chess.

Amy Pickett was famous for being quaint. She once found some white marbles in a drawer. They left a spicy smell on her fingers when she played with them. Amy put two and two together and decided the marbles were sweets. So she ate one. It tasted disgusting, of course. The white balls had been put in the drawer to kill moths.

Later on, when the doctor asked her how she had managed to do such a foolish thing, Amy showed him – by swallowing another. She was quaint like that.

When Clarice Cooper and her mother came to live in the village, people were still talking about Amy and the moth-balls. It upset Mrs Cooper. She began to worry about being next door to the Picketts. How was she going to protect her delicate Clarice from a rowdy little plumber's daughter who ate moth-balls?

Then a strange thing happened.

Early one morning, Mrs Cooper leaned out of her bedroom window and asked Mr Pickett, very politely, if he would please stop throwing bits of pipe into the back of his van.

'I can't stand noise,' she said.

'That's because you work in a library,' said Mr Pickett.

'You do this every morning,' said Mrs Cooper. 'It's noise pollution. It wears people down, like invisible grit.'

'Try being a quiet plumber,' said Mr Pickett.

And he went on throwing loud metal into his van.

Mrs Cooper lost her temper. She filled a bucket with water and emptied it over Mr Pickett from her bedroom window. He was so surprised, he could only stare at her with his mouth wide open.

He stood in a puddle in his wet overalls, hair dribbling all over his face, just gaping at her.

Then Mrs Pickett came out into the yard with a basket of washing to hang on the line. She took one look at the state of Mr Pickett and went back into the house again.

'Drat it,' she said. 'Rain wasn't forecast today.'

Wet Mr Pickett pulled a silly face at cross Mrs Cooper. He blew a drop of water off the end of his nose and did a little dance in the puddle. They both began to laugh. In fact, Mrs Cooper became so hysterical she had to sit down. When she recovered, she apologized to Mr Pickett for soaking him and Mr Pickett promised to try and be quieter with his pipes and tools. In no time at all, they were drinking tea together in Mrs Pickett's kitchen like old friends.

After that, Mrs Cooper stopped worrying about her neighbours. She grew accustomed to their free and easy ways. She even managed to smile whenever moth-balls were mentioned.

If Amy Pickett really *was* a chicken, it would not have surprised Mrs Cooper at all.

'My real mother,' said Amy, hopping about in School Lane, 'was a Rhode Island Red. She had ever such a pretty beak.'

'I'm fed up with this game,' said Clarice. 'Why can't you be Joan of Arc or the Prime Minister?'

When they got to the school, one of the older girls ran across the yard with a dustbin lid. She used it to push Amy and Clarice into a corner.

'I am a Warrior Queen,' she shouted, 'and you are my slaves.'

She waved the lid over their heads. 'This is my magic shield.'

'It's a bin lid,' said Amy and Clarice together.

Neither of them liked Betty Dibble. She was stronger than any of the boys in the school and everyone knew she tortured her dolls.

'Shut up, you,' she shrieked. 'Slaves can't talk.'

'Waaark, quaaark.'

Betty Dibble stopped being bossy long enough to give Amy a queer look.

'What's the matter with *her*?' she said.

'Please, Your Majesty,' said Clarice, 'she thinks she's a chicken.'

'Big deal,' said the Warrior, forgetting she was supposed to be royalty.

She pushed Amy against the wall. 'Chicken-in-a-basket, are you? Chicken with chips?'

'Cluck, cluck,' said Amy, rubbing her arm.

'And vinegar,' said Bossy Betty, pushing her

again.

'Cluck cluck, CLUCK!'

Then Miss Metcalfe came out onto the school steps to ring her bell.

'Inside, everyone,' she shouted, 'and no pushing.'

She swung the bell from side to side and up and down. The din was terrible. The way she shouted and carried on, you would never have suspected Miss Metcalfe of being a lady.

'Put that lid back, Elizabeth Dibble. We don't want wasps in Geography.'

They sang the Tuesday hymn before starting Geography. Miss Metcalfe banged away on the piano in the same wild way that she rang the handbell. She could only play five tunes, so the hymns never changed from week to week. Yesterday it had been Onward Christian Soldiers, with everyone yelling the words and marching on the spot. Tomorrow it would be Amy's favourite, There Is A Green Hill Far Away. The Tuesday hymn was called As Pants The Hart For Cooling Streams.

As usual, Clarice giggled when she sang 'pants'. For once, Amy was not amused.

'It's a well-known fact,' Clarice chanted, in

time to the words of the hymn, 'hens have no sense of humour.'

'Black mark, Clarice Cooper,' shouted Miss Metcalfe, trying to dig her fingers into the keyboard.

All through Geography, Amy made chicken noises. She scuffled about on the floorboards under her desk, pretending to scratch for grain. It got on Miss Metcalfe's nerves.

'Stand up, Amy Pickett.'

Amy clucked softly and rolled her eyes in a mad way.

'Are you sick, child?'

'Please, Miss,' said Bossy Betty, 'she's turning into a chicken.'

There was a silence. Someone tried to stifle a giggle.

'No human being,' said Miss Metcalfe, 'ever turned into a chicken. Although I can think of some who deserve to be put behind wire. Black mark, Amy Pickett. Sit down and be quiet.'

After that, Geography continued without inter-ruption until Amy suddenly raised her hand. Miss Metcalfe sighed.

'Now what?' she said. 'What now?'

'I have to lay an egg,' said Amy.

This time she had gone Too Far.

'Enough is enough,' said Miss Metcalfe. 'Two black marks and stand in the corner. I shall speak to your mother.'

'Serves you right,' said Bossy Betty during playtime. 'You're round the twist, you are. You're out to lunch.'

'Leave her alone,' said Clarice. 'She's feeling broody.'

'Watch my lips, Amy Pickett. You're SIMPLE.'

When school finished, Miss Metcalfe wandered about the empty classroom with a mug of tea. She enjoyed this part of her day almost as much as ringing the bell in the morning. There were only seventeen pupils at All Saints but by going-home time, Miss Metcalfe was glad to see the back of them all. (Sometimes she hoped that pupils like Elizabeth Dibble and Amy Pickett would stay away and not come back until they were about fifty.)

She found a sheet of paper under Amy Pickett's desk. It was covered in drawings of chickens: a fat one, a skinny one, a grinning chicken, an eating chicken and one chicken flying.

'That child,' she said to the rows of empty desks, 'is a problem. That child lives in a world

9

of dreams.'

She drank her tea and then telephoned Amy's mother, who was not in the least like a Rhode Island Red.

'That child,' she said, 'is going from bad to worse. I wouldn't like to tell you how she behaved in class today.'

She did, though, and in detail.

'She's been very peculiar in her manner, Mrs Pickett. It's not at all satisfactory. I won't have a chicken disturbing my class.'

'Well, who's been putting chickens in her head?' said Mrs Pickett.

'If she had a brain in her head, there wouldn't be room for chickens,' said Miss Metcalfe.

And she put down the telephone before Mrs Pickett could start an argument.

'I don't know what's got into you,' Amy's mother said to her at tea-time. 'Going on about poultry all the time.'

'What do you want to be a chicken for?' said Mr Pickett. 'It's not all beer and skittles, you know.'

'For a start,' said Mrs Pickett, 'hens don't get to eat lemon meringue pie for their tea.'

'My Uncle Percy thought he was a chicken,'

said Mr Pickett.

'Don't be silly, Trevor.'

'It's the truth.'

'That's it, then,' said Mrs Pickett. 'She's taking after your Uncle Percy.'

'More likely to take after you,' said Mr Pickett, who was on his second can of beer and feeling quite brave. 'You once put a tuna salad in the microwave.'

'What happened to your Uncle Percy?' asked Amy.

'We all kept quiet about it,' said Mr Pickett. 'We needed the eggs.'

Plumbers never take anything seriously.

By the end of the week, Amy had collected fourteen black marks. This was a school record.

What started as a game of pretence had got completely out of hand. Even Clarice began to avoid her. They would set off to school together but if

Amy walked, Clarice ran. And if Amy ran, Clarice walked. It was embarrassing to be seen with someone who made chicken noises and laid an imaginary egg every ten minutes.

Poor Miss Metcalfe usually celebrated the arrival of the weekend by treating herself to a three-course meal in a nice restaurant. She decided against it that Friday night – in case they had chicken on the menu.

Chapter Two

On Saturday morning, Amy's father shut himself away in the front room and a lot of telephoning went on.

'Who's he ringing?' said Amy, flapping about at the kitchen sink with a tea towel.

'Don't ask,' said Mrs Pickett. 'This house is all secrets lately.'

'There's still mustard on this one,' said Amy.

Mrs Pickett took back the plate and washed it again.

'It must be something special,' she said. 'He's got that look.'

Then she just stood there, both hands under water with the breakfast dishes, and gazed out of the window.

'A car,' she said. 'I think it's a car. I've always wanted a car. He's buying me a car for my birthday.'

'You can't drive,' said Amy.

'A shiny red car with furry seat covers and a matching spider for the back window.'

'How's he going to wrap a car?' said Amy.

When Mr Pickett came out of the front room, he was looking very pleased with himself.

'Just nipping out,' he said, but he went upstairs instead. 'Just going to change.'

'Not into a chicken, I hope,' Mrs Pickett called after him.

It was an awful joke but Mrs Pickett seemed to enjoy it. A frying-pan slipped from her fingers and splashed into the sink. She held onto the draining-board with two soapy hands and laughed right out.

'Not into a chicken,' she warbled. 'Ha! Ha! Ha!'

On the landing, Mr Pickett held his nose and pulled an imaginary lavatory chain. Amy hung up the tea towel and carried on with the washing-up.

'How do you get a shine on a non-stick pan?' she said.

That stopped the laughter right away.

'You're barmy, Amy Pickett. Give me that.'

She snatched back the frying-pan.

'Now I *know* you take after his Uncle Percy.'

Later that morning, Mrs Cooper drove into Murdoch to buy Mrs Pickett a birthday present. Murdoch was a large market town seven miles from the village. Mrs Cooper worked in the library in the High Street.

Clarice had asked to go with her.

'There's a magazine I want,' she said.

'Go and tell Amy she can come, too,' said Mrs Cooper. 'But I won't stand for any of that chicken silliness in the car.'

'Nor will I,' said Clarice.

All the way to Murdoch, Amy made up stories in her head to stop herself from clucking. She said nothing. Now and then, Mrs Cooper glanced at her anxiously through the rear-view mirror. She had never known Amy to be so quiet for so long. Clarice spent the time counting green cars. This stopped her from being travel sick. Counting dogs worked just as well. Or people wearing hats. Her all-time record was seven hats and nine-and-a-half dogs but that had been on a journey to London. The half was for a poodle that might have been a cat.

Mrs Cooper parked her car over the Arcade Shopping Centre in the middle of the town and took Amy and Clarice for a coffee at The Bijou Bite. While they queued up for a table, Amy thought she saw her father's van backing into the big covered market in the square. Then she saw the Warrior Queen and forgot about the van.

'I've seen Betty Dibble,' she said. 'Her hair's dyed.'

'Wonder what killed it?' said Clarice, concentrating on the Bijou cake trolley.

'DYED, pinhead! There were blonde streaks in it.'

'Gruesome,' said Clarice, deciding on an apple doughnut.

Bossy Betty generally hung about her father's farm all weekend, hiding from any work that had to be done or throwing stones at his pigs. But sometimes she hung about at the Murdoch bus station instead, jeering at boys and showing off her latest piece of jewellery.

'Keep away from that Dibble girl,' said Mrs Cooper. 'She's a menace.'

In the end, morning coffee turned out to be one cup of tea, two strawberry milkshakes and nothing off the trolley at all.

'Right,' said Mrs Cooper, paying the bill. 'Half an hour. And stay inside the Arcade. I'll meet you back here at eleven.'

Amy and Clarice wandered about the three floors of the Shopping Centre. Amy tried on Clarice's glasses for a while but kept steering to the left and bumping into people.

'God must've known about glasses when he invented humans,' said Clarice. 'That's why he put ears where they are.'

They tried to imagine ears on their wrists (good for listening round corners) or on their ankles (bad for baths and pulling up socks).

Then Amy bought a birthday card for her mother and Clarice found the magazine she wanted in the same place. Walking out of the shop, they came face to face with Betty Dibble.

'Well, well, well,' she said, 'if it isn't Attila the Hen.'

'I do like your hair,' lied Clarice. 'You've had it cut.'

'I know that, stupid,' said Betty. 'I was there when they did it.'

'Well,' said Clarice, 'have a nice day.'

She edged away from the shop, pulling Amy

with her.

'Remind me never to come this way again,' said Betty.

'Never come this way again,' said Amy.

'Thanks for reminding me, hen-face.'

Betty Dibble went into the shop. Amy and Clarice ran to the elevator.

'If that Warrior Queen ever falls in the canal,' said Amy, 'I hope it's on a Saturday. She'll sink straight to the bottom with those dreadful clunky ear-rings.'

'What on earth,' said Clarice, pointing, 'is that?'

In a boring corner of the ground floor, the same corner where dead leaves and litter collected in the winter, a small tent had appeared. It was square with a pointed roof, as if the inventor had been unable to decide whether to make a marquee or a wigwam.

'*That* wasn't here last week,' said Clarice.

The canvas was painted in red and black and yellow stripes which made your eyes go funny when you looked at it from a distance. Amy and Clarice walked round the tent until they found a hand-painted notice which was pinned over the entrance.

> MADAM MARVEL
> FORTUNE TELLER TO THE
> FAMOUS
> ENTER IF YOU DARE
> In aid of the church fete

The last sentence had been printed in such small letters you could barely see them.

'I dare you,' said Amy.

'We're not supposed to talk to anyone we don't know.'

'You're scared.'

'Only if we do it together,' said Clarice.

'One at a time,' said a squeaky voice from inside the tent, making them both jump. 'And you don't *have* to be famous.'

Amy and Clarice moved away from the corner.

'Go on,' whispered Amy.

'We're not old enough,' whispered Clarice. 'Anyway, I don't want my fortune told.'

'Well, I do,' whispered Amy, 'and I'm not going in unless you do.'

'Are you still there?' said Madam Marvel, her voice mysteriously dropping from a squeak to a growl. 'I haven't got all day.'

The walls of the tent wobbled as something

19

heaved about inside. Then a large hand appeared through the flap that covered the entrance. A large finger beckoned.

'What I don't know about the future,' said Madam Marvel, 'isn't worth knowing.'

Amy shoved Clarice forward.

'If I scream,' said Clarice, 'run for help. I saw hairs on that hand.'

She gave Amy her magazine to hold.

'Promise not to go away?'

'How can I stay here *and* run for help?' said Amy, but Clarice had already been swallowed up by the tent.

Chapter Three

Madam Marvel was an exotic creature to find in down-to-earth Murdoch on a Saturday morning. She wore a long gypsy dress of many colours. Her head and shoulders were covered by a tartan shawl and her face was hidden by a piece of black net. Hundreds of tiny sequins, like fish scales, had been sewn to the dress. There were fish scales on the net as well.

'Come forward, dearie,' she said. 'Come into my astral glow.'

She pointed to a stool and Clarice sat down.

There was a little rug on the floor of the tent and a table on the rug and a lamp on the table. The fish scales flashed and dazzled in the lamp-light. There was also a glass ball on the table, partly covered by a lace handkerchief. To Clarice, the ball looked suspiciously like an upturned goldfish bowl and Madam Marvel's astral glow smelled quite strongly of cigarettes.

'How much does it cost?' said Clarice, opening her purse. 'Is it less if you're only eight?'

Madam Marvel shifted her chair closer to the table and removed the lace hankie. She waved her large hands over the glass ball, like someone trying to clear steam from a saucepan.

'Worship the heavenly orb,' she moaned. 'My astral body is rising.'

She continued to moan, swaying from side to side.

'Hocus-pocus mumbo jumbo.'

Now and then, when Madam Marvel swayed too close to the lamp, Clarice caught a glimpse of her face through the veil. She had a moustache.

'Mumbo jumbo hocus-pocus.'

Clarice suddenly realized that she could hear nothing inside the tent but her own breathing and Madam Marvel's peculiar voice. They might have been sitting together in the middle of a desert instead of the Arcade Shopping Centre. A scream would have to be ear-splitting for Amy to hear it.

'I think I'll be going now,' she said. 'Thank you

very much.'

The chanting stopped at once.

'Just cross my palm with a pound, dearie, and you may ask two questions.'

'A pound,' said Clarice. 'That's a bit expensive, isn't it?'

'And your next question?'

Madam Marvel snatched the coin from Clarice's fingers before she could change her mind.

'That's not fair. It wasn't a proper question.'

'There's others waiting,' said Madam Marvel, tapping the table impatiently with Clarice's pound. 'Your second question, please.'

'What a fiddle. I want my money back.'

'Don't keep Madam Marvel waiting, dearie. She might lay a spell on you.'

'Lay a spell,' said Clarice, standing up. 'Don't make me laugh. *You* couldn't lay a table. Give me back my pound.'

'It's for charity,' said Madam Marvel, dropping the coin into a pocket of her skirt. 'If you don't want your second question, go away and stop pestering me.'

Once again her weird voice altered in mid-sentence from a high sing-song to a rough growl.

Clarice left the tent, very hot and bothered.

'What a cheat,' she said. 'It's just Mr Griffin dressed up and speaking in a silly voice.'

Mr Griffin was the fishmonger in Murdoch High Street.

'I saw his moustache quite clearly,' said Clarice.

Amy had been leaning against a wall, looking through the magazine.

'Witches have moustaches,' she said.

'She's not dressed like a witch,' said Clarice crossly.

'They don't *all* have pointy hats and broomsticks,' said Amy, handing the magazine to Clarice.

'Let's go. It's nearly eleven.'

'I haven't had my turn yet,' said Amy.

She lifted the flap and went into the tent.

'Not *another* little girl,' said Madam Marvel, stubbing out her cigarette under the table. 'What is this? A school party?'

'I haven't got time to sit down,' said Amy. 'How much does it cost?'

'One pound, dearie, to ask Madam Marvel two questions.'

'I haven't got a pound.'

'What *have* you got?'

Amy produced a handful of coins from a pocket

of her jeans and held them out. Madam Marvel took them all. They joined Clarice's pound.

'For that, dearie, you only get one question. Make sure it's a good one.'

She waved her hands over the glass ball.

'The heavenly orb reveals all. Hocus-pocus mumbo jumbo.'

Cigarette smoke swirled from one side of the tent to the other.

'The crystal-gazer is ready for your question now.'

'How do I learn to speak Chicken?' said Amy.

Madam Marvel swallowed too much astral glow and began to cough. Under the veil, she pressed the lace hankie to her moustache and coughed and coughed. Fish scales fell off her dress and glittered on the table. The heavenly orb threatened to roll away.

'A spell is cast,' she managed to say eventually, half-choked. 'From this moment you can speak Chicken. Now run along and practise on some poultry.'

Ten minutes later, Mrs Cooper drove her car out of the Shopping Centre and into the High Street. Amy and Clarice were sitting in the back but not very close together.

'Go on, then,' said Clarice. 'Speak to me in Chicken. *Say* something.'

'I don't see the point,' said Amy grandly. 'You wouldn't understand.'

'Because you can't, can you? Because Madam Marvel was just a big cheat. She was Mr Griffin dressed up.'

'What are you two muttering about?' said Mrs Cooper. 'Did you meet anyone this morning?'

'We met a load of nasty jewellery,' said Clarice. 'Betty Dibble was behind it somewhere. And the fat lady who sells papers had a chicken loose in her shop.'

'Oh, Amy,' said Mrs Cooper, 'haven't you stopped all that nonsense?'

'*And* we met Mr Griffin,' said Clarice, staring hard at Amy. 'The fishmonger.'

'Whoever you met,' said Mrs Cooper, 'it wasn't Mr Griffin.'

She steered her car round a lorry full of sheep.

'Mr Griffin left the country last year. He lives in Spain now.'

Quaint Amy sat back in the seat, beaming. Sensible Clarice began her search for dogs and green cars but she already felt sick.

Chapter Four

When Mrs Pickett woke up on Sunday morning, she could hear Mr Pickett clattering about in the kitchen. He was making a pot of tea.

'Happy Birthday to me,' she said, sitting up in bed.

She looked out of the window. What she hoped to see was a shiny new car with furry seat covers. Everything seemed as usual in the garden. The grass needed cutting, the cat was doing its business under Amy's swing and the door of the run-down caravan, abandoned by a previous owner of the house, still creaked to and fro on one hinge. There was no sign of a birthday present from Mr Pickett.

She put on her slippers and hurried downstairs,

not even stopping to clean her teeth. She unlocked the front door and stood on the step in her nightie. Mr Pickett's van was parked, as always, just inside the gate. It almost filled the yard. Mrs Cooper's car was squeezed up against the hedge in the lane. There was no new car.

'Silly,' said Amy behind her. 'The postman doesn't come on a Sunday.'

Mrs Pickett turned round, the wind blowing her hair in all directions like a Catherine Wheel.

'All your cards came yesterday,' said Amy.

'Best come inside,' said Mr Pickett, joining her. 'Vicar might see you in your nightie.'

'Happy Birthday,' they both said.

'How about a nice cup of tea?' said Mr Pickett.

'Lovely,' said Mrs Pickett faintly.

She came back into the house and closed the door. They all retreated to the kitchen.

Mr Pickett made tea twice a year, on Christmas Day and on Mrs Pickett's birthday. This operation involved getting a lot of water on the floor, tea-leaves across the draining-board and milk over Mr Pickett's dressing-gown. It was quite usual for crockery to be chipped or even broken.

One Christmas morning, Mr Pickett had tripped over the cat and dropped the tray. For days after that, Moses haunted the landing, licking sugar out of the carpet.

Mr Pickett claimed he could make tea in his sleep and Mrs Pickett guessed that he probably *did* make it with his eyes closed. Twice a year her kitchen looked as if a blindfolded chimpanzee had been let loose.

She opened birthday cards and gave them one by one to Amy, who propped them up on the dresser. She had two parcels to open as well, neither of them big enough to conceal even a very small car.

'That one's from Clarice and her Mum,' said Amy. 'I think it's a book.'

'It looks like a book,' said Mrs Pickett, trying not to tear the pretty paper as she peeled it off the oblong package. 'It *feels* like a book.'

It was a box of crystallized fruit.

'And this one's from me,' said Amy, handing her mother a squishy bundle of paper bound up with a lot of white sticky tape.

'Interesting,' said Mrs Pickett, turning it over and over as she searched for a way in.

After a short struggle with the tape, she unwrapped two woollen objects. They were coloured orange and pink and black.

'Good grief,' said Mr Pickett. 'Where are my dark glasses?'

'I knitted them myself,' said Amy.

Mrs Pickett pushed her fingers through several holes in the wool.

'They're smashing, love. Just like proper shop mittens.'

'They're egg-cosies,' said Amy, beginning to sulk. 'Clarice said there had to be holes to let the steam out.'

'And now for *my* present,' said Mr Pickett. 'Eyes shut, please.'

He opened the back door into the garden.

'In my nightie?' said Mrs Pickett, already in a great state of excitement. 'You'll get me arrested.'

'In your nightie *and* with your eyes closed.'

Guided by Amy, Mrs Pickett allowed herself to be taken out into the garden. She giggled when grass tickled her ankles. When they stopped, Mr Pickett turned her round and round until she felt dizzy.

'Now,' he said, 'are you ready for a big surprise?'

'Trev, you didn't,' said Mrs Pickett. 'Not a new car? Oh, Trev, you shouldn't have.'

'I didn't,' said Mr Pickett.

Mrs Pickett opened her eyes.

'There,' said Mr Pickett.

All she could see in front of her was the old caravan. 'What? Where?'

'Have a look inside.'

Mrs Pickett stared at her husband very suspiciously and then stared at the caravan. It was a nervous wreck. It had been stuck at the end of the garden for longer than anyone could remember, wobbling uneasily on stacks of bricks.

Mr Pickett had taken the wheels off to make a wheelbarrow. All the windows were broken and some had brambles growing through them.

'Go on,' he said, giving Mrs Pickett a little push.

'Is it a puppy?' said Amy.

'Guess again.'

At that moment there was a great din inside the caravan and something alive tumbled out onto Mrs Pickett's damp slippers. She gave a little shriek and stepped back.

'That,' she said, 'is either an elf with very poor dress sense or a large chicken.'

'Ten out of ten,' said Mr Pickett, smiling an enormous smile with a lot of teeth in it. 'Three, as a matter of fact.'

'Three chickens,' said Mrs Pickett in a choking voice.

'Couldn't wrap them,' said Mr Pickett. 'Wouldn't stand still long enough.'

Mrs Pickett opened her mouth and closed it again. Her eyes became very small. Her lips were so thin they practically disappeared. She was preparing to be very annoyed indeed.

'Let me get this clear, Trevor. You have bought me three live chickens for my birthday.'

'Just think,' he said, 'fresh eggs every morning.'

'And my egg-cosies,' said Amy, peering into the caravan.

In the gloom she could just make out Mr Pickett's garden tools, a few flower-pots and some faded deck-chairs. Then, when she looked up, she saw two chickens perched on the shelf where Mrs Pickett stored apples every winter. Amy blinked at them and they blinked back.

'Where did you get them, Trevor?'

'From the market.'

Mr Pickett had stopped being playful now and become quite flushed.

'Take them back, please. What am I going to do with three chickens? Where are they going to live?'

'Where they are, of course. They're Free Range.'

'All over my garden, you mean. Great idea, Trev. Really brill. Last year cows, this year hens. A lovely cow for my birthday, you said. Fresh milk, you said.'

'You didn't want a cow.'

'I didn't want chickens, either. I wanted a car.'

'Well, you got chickens instead. They're cheaper.'

'Let's keep them, Mum,' Amy pleaded. 'They can't go back for a fortnight anyway.'

'That's right,' said Mr Pickett. 'Poultry market's only twice a month.'

Mrs Pickett felt very tired and wished she had stayed in bed.

'I'm not having a lot of noisy, smelly chickens roosting in that caravan.'

'Where's the harm, woman? Amy's mad about chickens.'

'It's not Amy's birthday.'

It was clear now that she was going to be angry for some time.

'I'll look after them,' said Mr Pickett.

'You're a plumber,' Mrs Pickett shrieked. 'What you know about chickens I could write on a washer.'

She went back into the house and slammed the kitchen door.

'Blimey,' said Mr Pickett. 'It's the end of civilization as we know it.'

He went after Mrs Pickett and the kitchen door slammed again. In the silence there was a great din of insects. Then Amy picked up the chicken from the wet grass and tried to rearrange her feathers to lie in one direction.

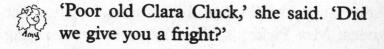 'Poor old Clara Cluck,' she said. 'Did we give you a fright?'

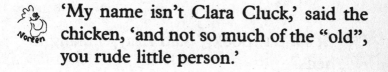 'My name isn't Clara Cluck,' said the chicken, 'and not so much of the "old", you rude little person.'

Chapter Five

Amy sat on the floor of the caravan, hugging her knees. Mrs Pickett's birthday present sat facing her, more or less in a row.

 'It's a bit spooky,' said Amy, 'talking to hens.'

The three chickens were at a loss for words.

 'It's Madam Marvel's magic,' explained Amy. 'She cast a spell.'

The chickens put their heads together and made a kind of sound impossible to write down.

At first glance they had looked the same. One bundle of feathers was very much like another – except to a chicken, of course. Now Amy could see the differences. There was an old chicken and a young chicken and one who was not quite either but very definitely overweight.

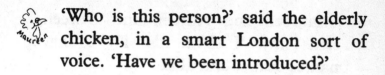

'Who is this person?' said the elderly chicken, in a smart London sort of voice. 'Have we been introduced?'

'Amy Pickett,' said Amy. 'Pleased to meet you.'

'You may escort me to my room, Amy Pickett,' said the elderly chicken grandly. 'I am exceedingly weary.'

'Just ignore her, clucky,' said the young chicken. 'She talks posh like that to everyone.'

'Are you the one I picked up?' asked Amy.

'No, she isn't,' said the fat chicken. 'I am.'

39

She still sounded very put out.

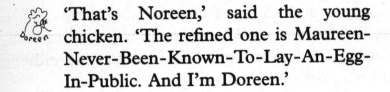

'That's Noreen,' said the young chicken. 'The refined one is Maureen-Never-Been-Known-To-Lay-An-Egg-In-Public. And I'm Doreen.'

'Maureen and Noreen and Doreen,' said Amy. 'I think it's silly to have names that sound alike.'

'Does she know *nothing* about chicken tradition?' said Maureen regally. 'This person is a fool.'

She stretched out a scrawny neck and sniffed at Amy's jeans, which had seen better days.

'You're a boy person, I suppose,' she said. 'You're too ghastly to be a girl.'

'I've got a sister called Pauline,' said young Doreen. 'And an auntie called Chlorine.'

'You can't call someone Chlorine,' said

40

Amy. 'It's what they put in swimming pools.'

 'That's right, clucky. A pretty perfume.'

 'Actually,' said Amy, 'a nasty disinfectant.'

 'The name Pickett's not exactly elegant,' said fat Noreen bluntly.

 'I didn't mean to be rude,' said Amy. 'It's just that it's hard enough already to know who's who.'

 'It's simple,' said the fat chicken, 'to anyone with half a brain. Maureen's a lady, Doreen isn't and I'm in charge. If that's still too hard for you to work out, you'd better call me Beryl.'

 'I have four cousins in Somerset,' said weary Maureen. 'Their names are Cora, Flora, Nora and Dora. Frightfully amusing.'

'What we want to know, Amy Pickett,' said fat Beryl, fluffing up her feathers in a businesslike manner, 'is what you're going to do about this dump?'

Immediately after breakfast next door, Mrs Cooper began to get lunch ready. She was peeling potatoes while Clarice's mouth was still full of toast and marmalade.

'I've run out of garlic,' she said. 'Pop round and ask Mrs P. And don't forget to say Happy Birthday.'

Mrs Cooper had invited the Pickett family to lunch. It was part of her present for Mrs Pickett, to go with the box of crystallized fruit.

So Clarice squeezed through the hedge between the gardens, expecting to find Amy or her father working on his van in the yard.

Mr Pickett seldom thought of anything on a Sunday morning except his van. He could spend hours tinkering under the bonnet or, flat on his back like a road accident, under the van. On fine days, Amy was allowed to wash it. She would plonk about in wellingtons, dragging a hosepipe

42

behind her and making huge puddles in the yard. Sometimes she made huge puddles in the van, too, if she forgot to wind up the windows first. She had to stand on a kitchen chair to get at the roof.

Neither Mrs Cooper nor Mrs Pickett ever hung anything out to dry (or set up a barbecue) on the mornings that Amy washed the van. The sun would be shining in a cloudless sky and then it would begin to rain five minutes after she put the hose away. Mrs Cooper said that was called Fate. Mrs Pickett called it something much ruder.

This Sunday morning, Clarice found the yard deserted. The silence was peculiar. Mr Pickett, according to Mrs Cooper, was the noisiest man she had ever met. He yelled and whistled and chucked bits of plumbing about. The whistling was especially annoying because he only seemed to know one tune. Today, though, a deathly hush had settled over the Pickett property.

For some reason, Clarice felt nervous about going into the house. She could sense that all was not as it should be. She hung about outside, just to be safe, hoping Amy might appear. She wrote WASH ME with her finger on the mucky van. She made up a scary story in her head about the whole family being poisoned by a box of crystallized fruit and then almost died of fright when the kitchen door suddenly opened. Mrs Pickett appeared, still in her nightie and clutching a teapot.

'Happy Birthday,' began Clarice, with a bright smile.

'Not now,' said Mrs Pickett, scowling at her. 'I'm not in the mood. If you want Amy, she's in the caravan.'

It was quite clear that she *was* in a mood. She tipped tea-leaves over a bucket of compost and went back into the house.

'Mum says . . .' said Clarice.

The kitchen door closed in her face. Sensibly, Clarice gave up and wandered over to the caravan.

Amy's face appeared at one of the broken windows.

'You can't come in,' she said dramatically.

'Who wants to?' said Clarice, losing her temper. 'I only came round for some garlic. I hate you, Amy Pickett. You're a silly big cow.'

There was a furtive scuffling sound from inside the caravan.

'What's that noise?'

'What noise?' said Amy.

'A silly big *deaf* cow,' yelled Clarice. 'You and your stupid secrets. You're funny in the head, Amy Pickett. You're a sandwich short of a picnic. The stairs don't reach the attic.'

'And you give me earache,' Amy yelled back.

Clarice had run out of insults. 'I'm going,' she said.

'Goodbye,' said Amy.

They glared at each other, their faces getting hotter by the second.

'Go on, then,' said Amy.

'I will,' said Clarice.

'Good,' said Amy.

Her face disappeared from the window. Clarice waited for the face to come back or for Amy to throw something at her. Nothing like that happened. Instead, she heard the scuffling sound again. A large brown feather floated out of a hole in the roof.

'If you're still there,' said Amy, 'you can come in.'

Clarice picked her way daintily over some brambles and looked in at the caravan door. When her eyes grew accustomed to the gloom, she could see fresh shoots growing through gaps

in the floor and tree roots that had wound themselves around the WC in a very unusual manner. Amy was sitting on a bunk with Doreen perched on her left and fat Beryl perched to her right. Maureen-Never-Been-Known-To-Lay-An-Egg-In-Public had taken up residence on the lavatory seat and was fast asleep.

Clarice was not impressed.

'Chickens,' she said, staring at the chickens. 'I might've guessed.'

'I can talk to them,' said Amy recklessly.

'Oh, don't start *that* again,' said Clarice.

She moved a rusty can aside and sat down in the doorway so that her feet dangled out of the caravan.

'This place pongs.'

'Mum stores apples in here. You'd better put that tin back properly. It's for catching drips when it rains.'

'What's the matter with your Mum?' said Clarice, swinging her legs. 'Is she ill?'

'I expect she's thinking about it,' said Amy.

Clarice looked confused.

'She's sulking,' said Amy and she told Clarice why.

'I don't blame her,' said Clarice. 'Who wants chickens for a birthday present? They make rotten pets. They can't fly. They can't sing. You can't take them for walkies.'

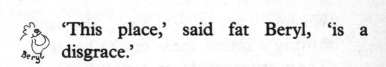 'This place,' said fat Beryl, 'is a disgrace.'

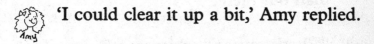 'I could clear it up a bit,' Amy replied.

'Don't start clucking again,' said Clarice.

'I was just chatting to Beryl,' said Amy.

'This place won't do at all,' said Beryl. 'We're not going to be treated like second-class poultry.'

 'A bit of paint,' said Amy, 'and some curtains.'

'I'm not playing this game any more,' said Clarice and went home.

 'We don't want curtains,' said Beryl. 'We don't want fitted carpets. We don't want musak. We're not demanding anything unreasonable.'

She began to march up and down the bunk in a militant manner, followed by a cloud of dust.

 'We just want a nice coop,' she said, shoving a rotten apple out of her way. 'There are more things growing in here than out there.'

 'What's musak?' whispered Doreen.

Amy shrugged. She had no idea.

48

'Is Beryl always so bossy?' she whispered back.

'Oh, don't mind her, clucky. She's only in charge because she's the biggest and the loudest. If she was a person, she'd be driving lorries.'

'I know someone like that,' said Amy, thinking of Betty Dibble.

'This place leaks,' said Beryl, raising her voice. 'It's a wind tunnel.'

'She's right, clucky,' said Doreen, admiring her own reflection in a piece of broken mirror. 'It's dead grotty in here.'

'Thank you, dear,' said Beryl severely. '*I'm* Senior Layer in here and *I'll* do the moaning.'

'Oooh!,' said Doreen, rolling her eyes. 'Pardon me for breathing. Queen Beryl's on the throne.'

'She's not the only one,' said Amy, nodding at Maureen.

The elderly chicken opened one eye and blinked back at her.

 'Musak,' she said grandly, 'is a kind of Greek stew. How ignorant the young are nowadays.'

 'As Senior Layer,' said Fat Beryl, 'I speak on behalf of my sisters. Until we're provided with proper living space and better conditions there will be no eggs.'

 'Chicken Lib! Chicken Lib!' chanted Doreen, carried away by the sound of the words. 'Chick-chick-chicken Lib!'

 'United we stand,' said Maureen primly, opening her other eye, 'divided we fall.'

Coming from a well-bred family, she was a hen with great self-control.

'My mum won't stand for that,' said Amy. 'She thinks you're useless already. United you stand. Divided you go in the oven.'

 'No threats, please,' said Beryl.

 'This coop co-op is now on strike,' cackled Doreen.

 'And please close the door on your way out,'saidMaureen-Never-Been-Known-To-Lay-An-Egg-In-Public. 'I feel one of my headaches coming on.'

Chapter Six

The thundercloud that had settled over the Pickett house spread wider during the morning until it covered the Cooper house as well.

First of all, Clarice came home in a temper. She slammed the back door.

'I hate Amy Pickett,' she said. 'She's worse than spinach.'

She marched past her mother, who was kneeling on the floor with her head in the oven, and slammed the kitchen door as well. Caught in the draft, gas burners in the oven gave a loud pop and a pretty blue flame took a fancy to Mrs Cooper's eyebrows. She withdrew her head in a hurry.

'It's not too late to have you adopted,' she shouted after Clarice. 'And where's that garlic?'

The only answer she got was the sound of another door slamming.

Ten minutes later, Moses squeezed through a window into the front room and found a bowl of trifle on the sideboard.

'Clarice,' yelled Mrs Cooper, after chasing the cat out of the house. 'Come down this minute and lay the table.'

Clarice came slummocking down the stairs. She dragged herself round and round the table, clattering cutlery and banging crockery, while her mother tidied up the trifle. It took Mrs Cooper

ages to pick all the black hairs out of the custard and by the time she got back to the kitchen, a pan of potatoes had boiled dry.

'I haven't the patience,' she sighed, beginning to feel that things were not going according to plan.

She put the scorched saucepan outside to cool down. During the afternoon the potatoes were carried away by an army of ants who probably thought it was Christmas.

The birthday lunch was not a success. Mrs Pickett was still hopping mad about the chickens, Amy was in a crabby mood and so was her father. Mr Pickett really hated dressing up but, to please Mrs Cooper, he had put on his best suit and a tartan tie. He felt half-strangled by the terrible tie. He was already scarlet in the face because he had shaved in a hurry at the very last moment and his cheeks were still in shock.

'Happy Birthday, Lucille,' said Mrs Cooper, dishing up the roast lamb.

'Now there's a novelty,' said Mr Pickett gloomily. 'Being happy on your birthday.'

'Oh, shut up, Trevor,' said Mrs Pickett.

That was how badly it began and it got worse. Chickens kept cropping up. None of them could leave the subject of poultry alone. It was like picking at a dry scab.

'Don't you come near me,' said Clarice, scowling at Amy. 'Chickens carry diseases.'

'You haven't got room for any more spots,' said Amy, 'Volcano Face.'

'I think chickens are stupid,' said Clarice. 'What's the use of having wings if you can't fly?'

'Actually,' said Amy, 'they *can* fly, actually.'

'No, they can't.'

'Yes, they can. I read this story once about some chickens and a fox. It kept sneaking up on them at night and eating them. So the hens that hadn't been eaten learned to sleep at the top of a tree. That's not stupid.'

'All I ever wanted,' said Mrs Pickett, looking depressed, 'was a nice little car with furry seat covers.'

'Perhaps next year,' said Mrs Cooper.

'Pigs might fly,' muttered Mr Pickett. 'Like chickens.'

Poor Mrs Cooper began to chatter away as if her life depended on it.

'When I was a little girl,' she said, 'all *I* ever

wanted was a rocking-horse. Or a musical-box. One year my parents asked me what I'd like for Christmas, so I told them – a rocking-horse or a musical-box. Guess what? They gave me a pin-cushion.'

'Believe me,' sighed Mrs Pickett, 'a pin-cushion's better than chickens.'

'I was so annoyed I ran all the way down Rosamund Street and threw it in the canal. It played a little tune as it sank. It was a musical-box as well, you see, and I hadn't realized. I cried and cried.'

Clarice, who had heard this story before, made a pattern on her plate with mashed potatoes and gravy.

'How do you know they *flew* up the tree?' she asked Amy.

'How else would they get up there, stupid?'

'They could've climbed a ladder.'

'Clarice,' said her mother, 'if you can't say something sensible, don't say anything at all.'

'In Egypt,' said Mr Pickett, chasing a Brussel sprout around his plate, 'some chickens live a lot better than their owners.'

This remark fell into the front room silence like a block of concrete into a small pond.

'Fancy that!' said Mrs Cooper feebly, once the ripples had settled down. 'Egypt!'

'Congratulations, Trevor,' said Mrs Pickett. 'That was very nearly interesting.'

'Mr Dibble's cows have all got names,' said Mrs Cooper. 'What are you going to call your hens?'

'Dinner,' said Mrs Pickett. 'I have this nice recipe for chicken done with bacon and mushrooms.'

'They're not pets,' said Mr Pickett as the Brussel sprout at last surrendered to his fork. 'They're here to lay eggs.'

'How lovely,' said Mrs Cooper, doing her best to be cheerful. 'Nice and fresh every day.'

'Anyway,' said Amy, 'they've already got names.'

'Barnyard Bertha,' said Clarice. 'Farmyard Fanny.'

Mrs Pickett cut up a piece of meat in a not very nice surgical way.

'My sister was right,' she said. 'I should've married Ivor Lloyd.'

'Pity you didn't,' said Mr Pickett.

'Oh, Trevor,' cried Mrs Cooper, 'you don't really mean that. Where would you be without

Lucille?'

'Africa,' said Mr Pickett.

After that, Mrs Cooper kept quiet for a while. Sometimes it is a mistake to be nice to people who are determined to have a row. Sometimes it is much safer to sit well back and let them get on with it.

Mrs Pickett helped her to clear away the dirty dishes after the first course.

'I'm fed up,' she said, when they were alone together in the kitchen. 'I blame Amy for all of this. Going on about chickens, day after day. Putting ideas in her father's head. I can't think what's happened to that child.'

'She was always a bit quaint, dear,' said Mrs Cooper, remembering the moth-balls. 'Didn't she feed her recorder to Mr Dibble's carthorse?'

'Why can't she run away from home?' said Mrs Pickett, losing her head completely. 'Other children run away from home.'

'Don't be silly, Lucille,' said Mrs Cooper, quite stiff with disapproval. 'This is all getting out of hand. What a lot of fuss about three chickens.'

'I'd *pay* her to run away,' said Mrs Pickett. 'As a matter of fact, I'd probably go with her.'

Then they went back to the front room for

the trifle and soon after that the Pickett family returned home. What with one thing and another, Mrs Cooper was glad to see the back of them. She did the washing-up in a state of nerves, sincerely wishing that chickens had never been invented.

'Sometimes,' she said to Clarice, who was licking out the trifle bowl, 'I don't understand that family at all. They should come with a book of instructions.'

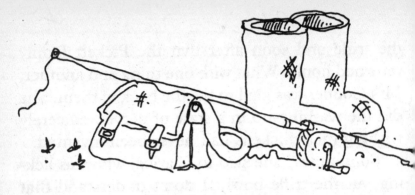

Chapter Seven

What should have happened next, like sunshine after rain, was a big kiss between Mr and Mrs Pickett, apologies all over the place and three fresh eggs for Sunday tea. Mrs Pickett would change her mind about her birthday present and admit that she really *loved* their fluffy bottoms and then Amy would run down the garden to the caravan to spread the good news. Everyone would live happily ever after.

What *did* happen next, like more rain after rain, was that Mrs Pickett locked herself in the spare bedroom. Wrapped in a duvet the size of a small elephant, she settled down to listen to a play on the radio. Mr Pickett, meanwhile, yanked his fishing-rod from a cupboard downstairs, slammed the front door on his way out of the house and tramped off in the direction of the river. He was still wearing his best suit and the terrible tartan tie.

Left alone, Amy hovered between the dirty van and the caravan. Right away, a few big splashy rain drops fell out of the tiniest of clouds. She only had to *think* about unrolling the hose pipe to bring on a downpour.

'Terrific,' bellowed Mr Pickett, clumping down Fairy Lane. 'Who needs umbrellas?'

Amy went into the house. Watched by a grumpy-looking Moses, she emptied a puddle out of his milk bowl and filled it again with bits of things from the fridge. There were bits of cold ham and bits of pastry and bits of yesterday's carrots. She crumbled a piece of cake over the top and made the meal really colourful with a dollop or two of tomato sauce.

By the time she had done this, Moses was very out of sorts (partly because he objected to his milk bowl being used for anything but milk and partly because he felt sick after guzzling so much cream off Mrs Cooper's trifle) and the mild little cloud over the village had been joined by a much angrier one. Rain drops were pinging off the filthy van quite musically.

'Great,' sighed Mr Pickett, getting wet on the river bank. 'How time flies when you're having fun.'

Amy ran across the garden, leaving a trail of sauce-stained pastry crumbs like little pink flowers in the grass. The three chickens had seen her coming and stood shoulder to shoulder in the caravan doorway.

 'Go away,' said blunt Beryl.

 'Go away,' echoed Doreen. 'What a nerve!'

If hens had hips she would have had her hands on them – if hens had hands.

 'Young person,' said Maureen, in a very superior voice, 'you should be prosecuted. Go away.'

 'Keep her out,' said fat, blunt Beryl. 'Girls, block her way!'

 'I'll peck her knees,' said Doreen.

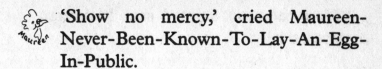 'Show no mercy,' cried Maureen-Never-Been-Known-To-Lay-An-Egg-In-Public.

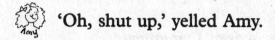 'Oh, shut up,' yelled Amy.

And she stepped right over Beryl and into the caravan.

'You stupid hens,' she said. 'I've brought you a meal.'

She dumped the bowl of food on the floor and sat down on a bunk. The rain got worse. Drops of water came through the battered roof but hardly any of them fell into the rusty tin on the floor.

'Did you see?' gasped Beryl, too shocked for a moment to carry on with her threatening behaviour. 'Did you see what she did?'

Maureen and Doreen blinked closely at the food in the milk bowl.

'How too, too dainty,' said Maureen, sarcastically.

 'Ugh!' said Doreen.

 'How disgusting! I smell cat.'

 'Sorry,' said Amy. 'It got a bit wet. If you want pudding, too, there's some crystallized fruit.'

 'I've gone right off carrots,' said Doreen.

 'A plate of primeval swamp,' said Maureen, retreating to the lavatory seat. 'I simply couldn't eat one mouthful. I already have indigestion.'

 'How can you talk about food,' Beryl screeched, flapping about in the doorway in a good imitation of a feathered windmill, 'when we're on a hunger strike?'

 'Oh, give it a rest,' said Doreen, tucking

in to a piece of ham. 'I'm starving.'

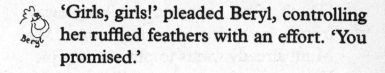

'Girls, girls!' pleaded Beryl, controlling her ruffled feathers with an effort. 'You promised.'

'Listen, clucky,' said Doreen, 'you may be on a diet but I'm a growing pullet.'

'I vote we take a vote,' said Beryl.

'I vote you take a running jump,' mumbled Doreen, her beak full of pastry.

'Manners,' said Maureen.

Lolling on the brink of the lavatory seat, she peered down at Beryl.

'A vote on *what*, precisely?' she asked, in the sort of voice you could crack eggs on.

'Whether to eat this person's food,' said the Senior Layer, pleased to be getting some attention at last, 'or go back to where we came from.'

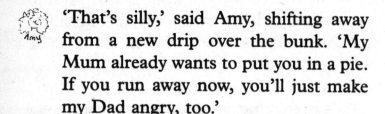

'That's silly,' said Amy, shifting away from a new drip over the bunk. 'My Mum already wants to put you in a pie. If you run away now, you'll just make my Dad angry, too.'

'We're Free Range,' said Doreen. 'We can go where we like.'

'No, you can't. You belong to us.'

'How dare you!' said Beryl, bristling with indignation. 'We're not your pets.'

'My Dad paid for you.'

'Not a man I'd care to be related to,' sighed Maureen, 'even by marriage.'

'We're not garden gnomes,' Doreen squawked, standing shoulder to shoulder with Beryl and enjoying the rumpus she was helping to make. 'We're not china ducks to be stuck on walls.'

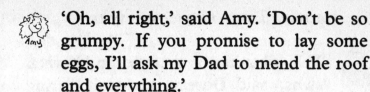

'Oh, all right,' said Amy. 'Don't be so grumpy. If you promise to lay some eggs, I'll ask my Dad to mend the roof and everything.'

'That's bribery,' said Beryl, who seemed determined not to see the bright side of anything.

'I give up,' said Amy, sliding off the bunk. 'What *do* you want?'

'Could you manage a small electric blanket, dear?' asked Maureen, with a very faint gleam of interest.

'You're barmy,' said Amy. 'I'm off.'

'I know what *I* want,' said Doreen. 'That big rooster from Bootlace Farm.'

Then she giggled in the way chickens do, which sounds a bit like a get-together of dead leaves in a draughty corner.

'Don't be so common,' said Beryl

67

primly. 'I won't have smutty talk.'

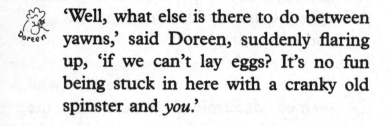

'Well, what else is there to do between yawns,' said Doreen, suddenly flaring up, 'if we can't lay eggs? It's no fun being stuck in here with a cranky old spinster and *you*.'

'Just a teensy-weensy electric blanket,' said Maureen, rocking back and forth on the lavatory seat.

'They call him Butch,' said Doreen, 'that rooster.'

'They call him Nigel,' said Beryl, 'and he's about as much fun as a weather-cock.'

And then they all started talking at once.

By the time her radio play ended, Mrs Pickett felt much better. She had managed to forget the chickens for two whole hours. She unrolled herself from the baby elephant on the spare room bed, tidied her hair a bit, unlocked the door and went downstairs to make tea.

Amy was standing by the fridge, drinking lemonade from the bottle. She had taken off her shoes but only after they had left a line of muddy prints across the kitchen.

Amy thought: *Use a glass, Amy.*

'Use a glass, Amy,' said Mrs Pickett, carrying the kettle to the tap.

Amy thought: *She always says that. Why does she always have to say that? I hate it when she says that.*

'I wouldn't always have to say that,' said Mrs Pickett, fetching the teapot from the dresser, 'if you used a glass.'

Amy screwed the top on the bottle and returned it to the fridge. Her mother immediately opened the fridge again to take out the milk.

'Heavens above, Amy!' she said, clutching the milk bottle and staring at what was left of a meat pie and salad supper. 'On top of that roast lamb and Brussels.'

'I fed the chickens,' said Amy, wondering which way to bolt if Mrs Pickett went on the rampage.

She headed in the direction of the open back door, pretending to skate there in her socks, zigzagging across the shiny cork tiles.

It had just stopped raining. The garden was dripping in watery sunlight. Interesting ponds had appeared where there had only been flower-beds before. The swing swung to and fro in a breeze and Moses sat under a shrub watching it, his head turning back and forth as if he was following a game of tennis.

Mrs Pickett sighed.

'What's the point?' she said, filling a jug with milk. 'Who's going to care in a hundred years that my garden's been turned into a farmyard?'

'Can we keep the hens, then?' asked Amy, zig-ging to the left and zagging to the right.

'Probably,' said Mrs Pickett. 'We'll see. Just as long as they know they're not here on holiday.'

Then she made the tea and Moses hypnotized himself in the lavender and Amy laid the table. And not so very far away, the wettest plumber in the country was chased by a goat across a field.

When he eventually got home, Mr Pickett looked like a street accident. The trousers of his best suit stuck to his legs as if they had been glued on the inside. All the colours in his painful tie had run, leaving a pattern on his shirt front the same shape as Australia. He also smelled quite ripe, having skidded in a cowpat and sat down in another one.

He stood dripping on the back doorstep and sniffed a lot.

'Catch any fish?' said Mrs Pickett over her cup of tea.

Mr Pickett, who had only hooked an old pram wheel and a lot of submerged weed, scowled at her through the draggly bits of hair that hung over his eyes.

'You went out fishing in your best suit,' said Mrs Pickett, cutting herself another slice of cake. 'If brains were dynamite, Trevor Pickett, you'd still go and blow your nose.'

Then she put down the cake knife and pushed her chair back and buried her face in her skirt. She laughed so much it hurt. She pointed, she gasped, she crossed her legs and hung onto the table.

'Ha! Ha! Ha!' she shrieked. 'No wonder your mother called you the Lincolnshire Handicap. Oh, dear!'

Mr Pickett dropped his fishing rod in the yard. He squelched into the kitchen and began to undress. First, he dumped the waterlogged jacket. Then he shuffled out of his boots and peeled off

his sticky trousers. He stood in his soaking shirt and underpants and socks and waited for Mrs Pickett to stop laughing.

Across the yard, Mrs Cooper and Clarice looked out from one of their windows.

'I don't expect the Common Sense Fairy ever got to his christening,' said Mrs Cooper. 'Or it could be something he's eaten.'

'Or the unleaded coffee,' said clever Clarice.

'Or decaffeinated petrol,' said her mother, who did crosswords. 'Don't look, Clarice. Goodness knows what he'll take off next.'

And they went back to watching television.

Chapter Eight

In the morning, Clarice had forgotten that she was never going to speak to Amy Pickett again.

'Coo-ee,' she yelled, scattering books and pencils down the lane in her scramble to catch up.

Amy, who was never in a hurry to get to school on a Monday, waited for her to retrieve everything. Then Clarice, who was tired out anyway after watching too much television the night before, sat on a wall and tweaked things about in her satchel as if next week would do.

'Your Dad's batty,' she said.

Amy agreed.

'My Mum says it's like living next door to a cartoon,' said Clarice.

'My Mum says she picked a lemon in the

Garden of Love,' said Amy.

'Doesn't he know anything else to whistle besides Yellow Submarine?'

Clarice polished her glasses and immediately Monday looked a lot cleaner and ready for use.

'We're sick of Yellow Submarine,' she said.

Mr Pickett's van came rattling down the lane. He leaned out of the driver's window and yelled at them as he went past.

'Girls who loll on walls deserve a Bad End!'

'Give us a lift, then,' Amy shouted.

'Sorry!'

The van turned a corner but Mr Pickett's voice blew back at them across the hedge.

'Emergency call. Billy Mullins again!'

Billy Mullins was only three years old but more trouble to a plumber than a dozen burst pipes or blocked drains. He was forever putting his Grandad's artificial leg in the washing machine and then pressing the buttons to give it a good seeing to.

'Your Dad's a lemon,' said Clarice, strapping up her satchel.

'Nobody's perfect,' said Amy.

And they walked on together.

'Old Grandad Mullins,' said Clarice as they

turned into School Lane, 'I wonder if he'll have his leg buried with him when he dies?'

'I expect they'll keep it for someone else to use,' said Amy.

'Is that what they do with false teeth?' asked Clarice.

'Ugh!' said Amy. 'Imagine having to use Miss Metcalfe's teeth to eat with.'

When they walked into the school yard, Miss Metcalfe's teeth were shouting at them to hurry up while the rest of her rang the bell.

As was usual on a Monday, Bossy Betty arrived late, barging into the middle of Onward Christian Soldiers.

'Black mark, Elizabeth Dibble,' said Miss Metcalfe as everyone settled down for Nature Class. 'Not a good start to the week.'

'Couldn't get my welly on, Miss,' Bossy Betty answered back with a smirk. 'Think someone left a foot in it.'

'This morning,' said Miss Metcalfe, when the giggling fizzled out, 'we're going to talk about plants.'

She dived into a shopping bag under her table and came up for air with a little flowering shrub in a pot.

'Does anyone know what this is called?'

There was a lot of sniffing and shuffling in the classroom. The shrub quivered on Miss Metcalfe's table, a mass of delicate pink bells all silently ringing. Then a boy put up his hand.

'Yes, Pepe?'

'A tulip, Miss.'

'Don't be silly.'

'A wallflower,' said someone else.

'My Daddy talks to flowers,' said Melanie Watts, a very pretty child who was bound to get married five minutes after she left school and live in the neatest house anyone ever saw with her rich husband and her clever children and the only dog in the county without fleas. 'He says it helps them to grow.'

'I bet he doesn't warn the grass before he cuts it,' said Clarice.

'We have a gardener to mow our lawn,' said Melanie, arranging her delicious blonde curls like bunches of grapes over each ear.

'Well, pardon us for breathing,' said Betty Dibble in a lah-di-dah voice.

'This plant is called a fuchsia,' said Miss Metcalfe. 'Pronounced few-sha. Can anyone spell that word?'

Amy stopped listening and drifted off into a daydream. She wondered what was going on in the caravan. The chickens had still been asleep when she left for school, huddled together on a bunk with their backs to the light.

'Still no eggs,' Mrs Pickett had grumbled at breakfast. 'Those birds are useless. We'd be better off with goldfish. At least they look pretty.'

'Hens need time to settle in,' said Amy.

'All of a sudden you're an expert on poultry,' said Mrs Pickett, attacking half a grapefruit as if it might still be alive.

'I've been talking to them.'

'Did you hear that, Trevor?' Mrs Pickett shouted.

Mr Pickett was pulling on his overalls in the yard but the back door was wide open.

'First she's pretending to be a chicken, then she's *talking* to them. Where's it all going to end? They'll put her in a padded cell. We'll be in the Sunday papers! I can see the headline now. PLUMBER'S DAUGHTER LAYS EGG.'

'It's no yolk,' said Mr Pickett, winking at Amy.

He ducked just in time. Half a grapefruit hit the side of his van.

'Pay attention, Amy Pickett,' said Miss Metcalfe. 'What did I just say?'

'Please, Miss,' Clarice interrupted. 'There's a man in the yard.'

There was a stampede towards the window, books flying, but Miss Metcalfe got there first. Eighteen pairs of eyes studied the stranger through steamed-over glass.

He stood in the middle of the yard and blew his pudgy little nose.

He was not a very exciting individual to stare at, being rather short, rather fat and rather bald. His brown suit looked as if it had been made by someone who bore him a grudge. It was tight in all the wrong places. He carried a briefcase in one hand and an umbrella in the other.

Miss Metcalfe sighed.

'As if I hadn't got enough to worry about. Go back to your desks, all of you. Open your books and keep quiet. And stop eating crisps, Elizabeth Dibble. You've just had breakfast.'

She tapped on the glass and made signs to the man in the yard. Then she left the room to go and meet him at the main entrance.

Amy and Clarice exchanged a glance. Clarice seemed about to say something but changed her mind when she saw Bossy Betty watching her.

Amy sat down at the desk and pondered. Something about the stranger reminded her of apple doughnuts and the Murdoch Shopping Centre. Perhaps Clarice had felt that, too?

In fact, it was the man's moustache which had seemed oddly familiar to Clarice. It put her in mind of a piece of limp seaweed under a pink pebble.

'Pay attention,' said Miss Metcalfe, returning almost immediately with the visitor beside her. 'This is Mr Arnold, the School Inspector.'

'Good morning, boys and girls,' said Mr Arnold, laying his briefcase and umbrella across Miss Metcalfe's table.

'Good morning, sir,' they chorused.

'What a fine little shrub,' he said, beaming at Miss Metcalfe's pot plant. 'One of God's prettier creations.'

'Please, mister,' said Pepe Jones, who was silly enough to believe that bananas have bones in them, 'did God make everything?'

'Of course,' said Mr Arnold.

'Even spinach?'

Miss Metcalfe groaned.

'Even spinach,' said Mr Arnold.

'Even the dentist?'

'Naturally.'

Miss Metcalfe thought: *I wish I worked on the buses. Being a teacher is a waste of time.*

This was the sort of thing she only thought when she was Very Gloomy Indeed.

'Even council houses?' asked Betty Dibble.

'Even Betty Dibble?' said Amy.

Behind Mr Arnold's back, Miss Metcalfe picked up her Black Mark Register and waggled it about as a silent threat.

'I hope you've all been working hard, girls and boys,' said Mr Arnold. 'You'll never amount to anything if you don't work hard.'

He began to move about between the desks.

'Well, young lady,' he said, pausing beside Betty Dibble. 'And what do *you* want to do when you leave school?'

'Take early retirement,' she said.

'Black mark, Elizabeth Dibble,' said Miss Metcalfe, banging the Register on the table and making everyone jump. 'Make that two. One for eating crisps in class and one for cheek.'

'And what exactly is a Black Mark?' asked the School Inspector.

'I award them for bad behaviour,' said Miss Metcalfe, giving the Dibble girl a steely look.

'Anyone with more than ten at the end of term is punished. Anyone with more than twenty marks is *severely* punished.'

'And anyone with more marks than that?' said Mr Arnold.

'Is in very serious trouble,' she said.

'Please, Mr Arnold,' said Melanie, putting on airs, '*I'm* going to be a champion knitter. I want to be the best knitter in the world and knit like nobody else ever knitted before. I'd like to win the Nobel Prize for knitting.'

Fortunately, Melanie Watts suffered from a speech impediment – she had to stop talking to draw breath – and Mr Arnold was able to move on before she began to prattle any more about knitting.

'Tell me, boys and girls,' he said, 'do you know why I'm here?'

'You're a Snivel Servant,' said Bossy Betty.

'*Civil* Servant,' hissed Miss Metcalfe. 'Sit up straight, Elizabeth Dibble.'

'It's Madam Marvel,' Clarice said loudly, in a sudden burst of recognition. 'I can smell the astral glow.'

There was a moment of shocked silence. Even Bossy Betty stopped eating crisps.

'Really, Clarice,' said Miss Metcalfe, wishing the floorboards would open up and swallow her.

She tried to smile at Mr Arnold but her cheeks refused to do what they were told. The lower half of her face just wobbled in a very peculiar way. She made up her mind to strangle Clarice Cooper after school.

'Where would we be without a sense of humour,' said Mr Arnold, although he was not himself laughing fit to bust. 'I'm sure I've never been a Madam Anything, little girl.'

'Yes, you have,' Amy shouted. '*And* you wore a dress on Saturday.'

After that, of course, there was a terrible racket. Amy might just as well have let off a firework in the classroom. All the girls giggled and snorted and shrieked, pointing at Mr Arnold. All the boys stamped their feet and chanted: 'Madam Marvel! Madam Marvel!', banging their desk lids up and down. Pepe Jones was so excited he widdled in his shorts. (This had happened before. His friends already called him PeePee Jones.)

For the first time in her life, Miss Metcalfe lost control. The louder she shouted for quiet, the worse the din became.

'Hocus-pocus,' screeched Amy. 'Mumbo

jumbo.'

Miss Metcalfe collapsed into her chair and hid her face in her hands. To have lost control was bad enough but to have done it in front of the School Inspector was a disaster.

She thought: *My life is a battlefield. I hate children. I wish I was at home with a nice cup of tea and a chocolate digestive.*

Mr Arnold took charge. First he shouted at Melanie Watts, who was making less of a racket than anyone else.

'Teacher isn't feeling well! Run and fetch a glass of water.'

Then he picked up the bell from Miss Metcalfe's desk and walked around the room ringing it until he was the only person making a row. Absolute peace was only restored when the bell was back on the table and Betty Dibble had climbed down from her desk.

'You and you,' said Mr Arnold, indicating Amy and Clarice and looking very hot under the collar, 'wait outside and don't make a sound.'

For one frightful moment it seemed as if they might refuse to move. Then Clarice rose with a sigh and left the room. Amy followed, sending out indignant thought waves in the School Inspector's direction.

'The rest of you,' he said, closing the door behind Amy, 'will sit quietly at your desks and write out one hundred times: MR ARNOLD DOES NOT WEAR A FROCK.'

Soon after that, Melanie Watts arrived back from the errand of mercy, her pretty curls all over the place.

'Only I couldn't find a glass,' she confessed, opening her heavenly blue eyes very wide, 'so I used this thingy from the cloakroom.'

Miss Metcalfe drank all the water, doing her best not to swallow any of the petals left in the vase.

Chapter Nine

'Now we've done it,' said Clarice. 'We've done it now.'

'Let's do a bunk,' said Amy.

'You're a panic, you are, Amy Pickett. We're in enough trouble already.'

They were standing in the corridor outside the classroom. Every now and then they could hear Mr Arnold clear his throat or a chair scraping or chalk squealing on the blackboard.

'*You'll* probably get the blame,' said Amy, at the end of another hundred years. 'They *expect* people like me and Betty Dibble to behave badly.'

'Thanks a bunch,' said Clarice.

'You're supposed to be the sensible one and set a good example.'

'Magic!' said Clarice miserably.

'I expect they'll send you to a place for school criminals. You'll have to share a toothbrush.'

'I've changed my mind,' said Clarice. 'Let's do a bunk.'

Ten minutes later they were recovering under an oak tree in the churchyard.

'You've broken my leg,' Amy grumbled, rubbing a very small graze on her shin.

Instead of fading away from the school like shadows, they had made enough noise to waken the dead. Clarice had fallen out of the cloakroom window on top of Amy. Then they had tried to squeeze through a gap in the wall together and tumbled into a hole on the other side that went down as far as Australia.

'You're not exactly Fairy Lightfeet,' said Amy. 'Why didn't you just walk out the front and slam the door?'

'All right, Clever Clogs,' said Clarice, pretending to be a brass rubbing, flat on her back with clasped hands. 'What are we going to do now? My mum will kill me.'

'They'll send out a search party,' said Amy, watching an earwig tramping through Clarice's hair, 'with sticks and dogs and policemen in blue

cardies, like on the telly. We'll be found just before teatime in a railway tunnel.'

'What railway tunnel?' said Clarice. 'You're barmy.'

Amy stopped daydreaming when she remembered they had left their lunchtime sandwiches behind.

'I bet Bossy eats them,' she said.

Clarice sat up and cleaned her spectacles. She looked around and shuddered. Some of the roots of the oak tree had risen to the surface like varicose veins.

'Let's go home,' she said, beginning to fret.

'It's only half-past ten.'

'I'm not mooning around in graves all day. It isn't healthy.'

'Suppose we're seen?'

'Say we're on a nature project,' said Clarice.

So they picked a few interesting weeds, to show anyone who might ask, and went home.

Poor Miss Metcalfe took some time to pull herself together after the riot. First of all she had been furious, blaming everyone but herself. While the School Inspector sat beside her, thumbing through the Black Mark Register, she had watched the little horrors writing out their lines and planned her revenge.

She would keep them all in after school, every day for the rest of the week. She would give Clarice Cooper ten black marks for causing the uproar. And another ten for making silly remarks about Mr Arnold's astral glow. And *another* ten because Clarice was her favourite pupil and this bad behaviour had been a terrible disappointment.

Then she began to feel twinges of guilt. Surely

an experienced teacher should be able to keep a few rowdy children under control? All it took was a firm voice and common sense.*

'This A. Pickett,' said Mr Arnold, leaning towards her and speaking softly, 'has a very impressive collection of black marks.'

'She gives chicken impressions,' Miss Metcalfe whispered back. 'In class.'

And right there and then she got over her attack of the jitters and began to blame Amy for everything.

Amy Pickett was a pest who ate moth-balls. Amy Pickett allowed a carthorse to chew her recorder. She was a Bad Influence on nitwits like Melanie Watts. She fooled about all day making poultry noises.

'Pickett,' said Mr Arnold, 'is a very good name for a chicken, if you think about it. Pickett! Pickett!'

Miss Metcalfe had no intention of thinking

* It is a well-known fact that some very bright people have no common sense at all. They may be able to solve mathematical problems in a flash and spell peculiar words like fuchsia and even recite verses in Latin but give them a milk carton to open and just watch them fall apart. Some very bright people would have difficulty getting into a packet of sliced bread without detailed instructions!

about it. If the School Inspector was going to imitate hens as well, she decided it was time to take charge again.

'Morning break!' she announced, standing up. 'I want everybody out in the fresh air.'

'And I must leave you, too,' said Mr Arnold.

He slipped a scrap of paper in between two pages of the Register, as if to mark his place, and then closed the book.

'A very interesting morning this has been,' he said, reaching for his briefcase and umbrella.

'It's a great shame you're *not* Madam Marvel,' said Miss Metcalfe. 'I'd arrange for you to cast a spell on that dratted Pickett girl. *She's* to blame for all the trouble this morning.'

'I'd be happy to oblige,' said Mr Arnold.

Betty Dibble's smirking face suddenly reappeared from the corridor.

'Please, Miss,' she said, 'I think they've done a bunk.'

'Nonsense,' snapped Miss Metcalfe. 'They can't do that.'

'They done it,' said Bossy Betty. 'It's did.'

A search party was organized, to make absolutely certain that Amy and Clarice were not hiding somewhere on the premises. And while everyone else was stampeding about, opening cupboards and looking under benches, only Pepe Jones saw the School Inspector slip quietly away. He watched the man pause in the yard to blow his nose again.

As Mr Arnold unfolded his handkerchief, a tiny shower of glitter fell from it, sparkling in the sunshine like fish scales. It was a nifty trick and it made Pepe smile.

Much later in the morning, during a spelling lesson, Miss Metcalfe opened up the Register to record yet another punishment and Mr Arnold's marker slipped out from between the pages. She only gave his doodle the briefest of glances before brushing it off the table into a waste-paper basket.

If she had taken a closer look, she would have found that the scrap of paper was covered in mysterious little pencil designs. And right in the middle of this weird diagram, Mr Arnold had printed the words: PICKETT INTO PULLET.

There had been nothing to disturb Amy and Clarice when they got home. Even Moses was curled up asleep under a bush.

Mrs Cooper, of course, was working in Murdoch Library and would be there until the afternoon. Mr Pickett was out somewhere with his van, perhaps still tinkering with the sabotaged washing machine. And Mrs Pickett's bicycle was missing.

'She could come back any minute,' said Clarice.

'No, she won't,' said Amy, making them both a cheese and pickle sandwich in her mother's kitchen. 'She's keeping fit.'

Mrs Pickett bicycled down to the Village Hall for a Keep Fit class every Monday morning. She jumped about to music and enjoyed a good wobble with her friends.

'Why doesn't she walk?' asked Clarice. 'The Village Hall's just round the corner.'

'She walks home,' Amy explained, 'but she's so fagged out she needs the bike to lean on.'

She thrust a lumpy sandwich at Clarice, picked up her own and went out into the garden.

Maureen-Never-Been-Known-To-Lay-An-Egg-In-Public had half buried herself in a flower-bed by the caravan. She was so still that Amy thought for a moment that she might actually be dead. Then she woke up with a loud squawk, remembered where she was and began to flutter about feebly in the dry earth. Little clouds of dust, like smoke, floated up around her.

'One of your chickens is on fire,' said Clarice.

'She's having a dust-bath, stupid.'

Amy crouched down. 'Good morning,' she said in Chicken.

Maureen stopped fluffing her feathers and let the dust settle.

'One wastes so much time,' she said, 'trying to stay beautiful.'

Clarice sat down on the swing and listened to Amy clucking. Sometimes she got fed up with making allowances. Sometimes it gave her a pain, being the best friend of a crackpot.

The elderly hen stood up unsteadily and stepped from the hollow in the flower-bed.

'It's high time my feathers were smooth again.'

'They look lovely,' lied Amy.

 'And are we not to be introduced?' said lofty Maureen, picking her way around the swing. 'Who is this person with pickle on her chin?'

'Maureen wants to meet you,' Amy said to Clarice.

The expression on Clarice's face would have turned milk sour.

'Who wants to meet a scrawny old hen?'

Amy was indignant. 'Don't start moaning,' she said, 'because I'm talking Chicken. I don't get nasty when you speak French. Chicken's just another foreign language.'

'Nobody understands Chicken except you.'

'Other chickens do,' said Amy.

Then Doreen appeared in the caravan doorway.

 'That bossy little madam's here again,' she announced over her shoulder.

A loud theatrical moan arose from the gloom behind her.

'What's wrong with Beryl?' said Amy.

 Doreen winked. 'Clucky, she's been like this since eggs was ten pence a dozen.'

 'I expect she has a cold,' said Maureen. 'Her age is catching up with her.'

 'I've got two colds,' said Beryl crossly, poking her head out of a broken window. 'There's a hurricane blowing through here.'

She glared down at Amy.

 'Where's our straw and our grain. A hen-house isn't decent without straw and grain. I don't see any straw or grain out here. We need grain to scratch in.'

Clarice sighed. Life would be simpler if she went about with someone fancy like Melanie Watts. Melanie was much kinder and prettier than Amy. Melanie told the truth and was never rude. In fact, she smiled so much it made your jaw ache just looking at her. Melanie even had a pony.

She gave in with another sigh, knowing very well, in spite of everything, that Amy was more fun to be with than anyone else in the village. Nice Melanie Watts was so wet you could empty her into a jug.

'Why are they in such a stew?' she asked.

Amy moved away from the caravan, where the three chickens were now all talking at once.

'Well,' she said to Clarice, joining her by the swing, 'there's good news and there's bad news.'

'Let me guess,' said Clarice. 'They're going on holiday but they want you to pay for it.'

Then she got off the swing and walked away.

'I'm off,' she said, 'before your mum comes home.'

'The good news,' said Amy, going after her, 'is that they've agreed to lay eggs if they get a load of straw.'

'Wow,' said Clarice, in a funny sort of mood. 'Terrific.'

'The fat one's coming with us,' said Amy, 'to make sure we get the best kind of straw. That's the bad news.'

'Us?' said Clarice.

'We?' she said, stopping so suddenly that Amy ran into her. 'What do you mean, *us*?'

She turned on Amy, ready for trouble.

'I'm not going anywhere with you and a stupid fat chicken.'

'Please,' pleaded Amy, her difficult gingery hair flying about in the wind. 'I can't do it on my own.'

'Do what?'

Amy took a deep breath and then spoke in a rush.

'If we go now we can be there and back before Bossy gets home from school.'

It was a moment before sensible Clarice understood what Amy was saying. When she did, she forgot the strange cross mood she was in and her dark face turned a shade paler.

Bootlace Farm!

To ask a local farmer for a sackful of straw for your chickens would be the simplest thing in the world – unless that farmer was a holy terror called Dibble with a wife and daughter to match.

Clarice shuddered. 'You're barmy, Amy Pickett.'

'There's nowhere else round here to get it from,' said Amy.

Clarice had once caught a glimpse of Bossy Betty's father, on market day in Murdoch. She had never seen such a huge man. From a distance he looked like a bus-shelter in breeches.

'We could take the bus,' said Amy.

'With a chicken?' said Clarice. 'Get serious.'

Which is more or less what bold Doreen was saying to fat Beryl at precisely that moment in the caravan.

 'How?' she said. 'In a shopping-bag?'

 'Certainly not.'

 'How undignified,' said Maureen. 'The very idea.'

 'On a lead then, like a dog?'

 'I wouldn't lower myself,' said Beryl.

 'Why can't we all go?' asked Doreen.

 'I'd never be up to the trip,' said Maureen sadly. 'My headaches, dear – I'm a martyr to them.'

 'Nobody asked you, anyway,' muttered Beryl.

'But I do think it might be a nice outing for Doreen. One does feel obliged to be generous to the less advantaged, doesn't one?'

'I'm in charge,' said Beryl regally. 'I'm going on my own and that's that.'

Chapter Ten

There was a bus-stop on the corner, where Fairy Lane joined the main road to Murdoch. Amy and Clarice went there in single file, keeping low behind a hedge in case they ran into Mrs Pickett.

They only met cattle on the way.

'Coochy-coochy coo,' said Clarice to a cow that strayed too close.

A blast of warm breath steamed up her glasses.

Clarice was still fairly new to the countryside. Anything alive that was larger than a dog made her cautious. Anything that dribbled and looked as if it had hard corners made her very nervous indeed.

'How do you stop a cow from charging?' she said.

'Take away her credit card,' said Amy.

'Moo,' said the cow, which as far as Clarice was concerned meant 'Get lost!' in beast language.

All Mrs Pickett would have seen from the other side of the hedge, if she had chosen that time to come toiling back with her bicycle from the Village Hall, was her very expensive London hat moving along above the hawthorn. And a fat chicken roosting in it.

The hat was on Amy's head.

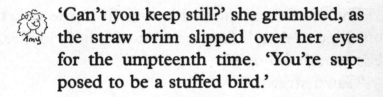

'Can't you keep still?' she grumbled, as the straw brim slipped over her eyes for the umpteenth time. 'You're supposed to be a stuffed bird.'

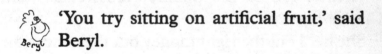

'You try sitting on artificial fruit,' said Beryl.

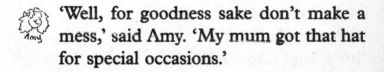

'Well, for goodness sake don't make a mess,' said Amy. 'My mum got that hat for special occasions.'

At eleven o'clock precisely, a bus appeared at the top of the hill and swept down on Clarice like a storm. Only when it stopped did Amy appear from behind a tree. The conductor who barely glanced at the girls when they boarded, followed them down the aisle.

'Any more fares?' he asked in a very bored voice.

Amy lowered herself onto a seat as if she had a glass of water on her head.

'Two returns, please,' she said, quite forgetting the straw they would have to carry home.

'Where to, love?'

'Back here, of course.'

The conductor raised his eyes from the ticket machine to Amy's face – and then a little higher. His mouth fell open.

'Gawd strewth!'

'Two *singles* to the Spinney crossroads,' said Clarice hastily.

She held out the right money but the conductor ignored it. He gaped at Beryl and Beryl stared back, trying hard not to blink.

'Is that a chicken?'

'It's a hat,' said Clarice.

'Stuffed,' said Amy.

'Language!' said the conductor.

'The *chicken's* stuffed,' said Clarice. 'It's for a school project.'

'You stuff chickens?'

'All the time,' said Amy, getting carried away. 'And turkeys. And goats.'

Clarice kicked her hard on the ankle.

'Well, I'll go to the foot of our stairs,' said the conductor, who was clearly scandalized. 'Where's the sense of it? Never happened in my day.'

He grabbed Clarice's money and punched out two tickets.

'Whatever happened to reading,' he said, 'and writing and arithmetic?'

He gave Beryl another sideways glance and went off down the aisle, shaking his head and muttering. Clarice sat as stiff as a stick and silently prayed that Mrs Pickett's wedding hat was keeping still, too.

'Goats,' she hissed from the corner of her mouth. 'You're off your hinges, you are.'

There were only two other passengers and neither of them appeared to have noticed the chicken on Amy's head. One man was reading a newspaper and another was snoozing. Lulled by the rocking and swaying and the steady drone of the engine, Beryl began to doze as well.

She was fast asleep, fortunately, by the time they reached the stop on Market Hill. A large poster had been stuck onto the bus shelter, advertising a new Chicken Take-Away in Murdoch. Amy nudged Clarice. She made frantic signs with her eyes.

'I think it's having forty winks,' whispered Clarice after a swift investigation of the hat.

'Right now,' Amy whispered back, 'I'd rather be doing multiplication. This is getting on my nerves.'

'It was your brilliant idea,' whispered Clarice, showing no mercy.

She felt like a criminal engaged in a Fowl Deed. *Do not pass Go. Move directly to jail.*

At the next stop they were joined by an old woman with a skinny brown dog. She sat down by the door and let go of the animal while she paid for her ticket. It wandered up the aisle, trailing a lead, until it found a piece of dead chewing-gum to lick. Then it clambered onto the seat in front of Amy and bared its teeth.

'Shoo,' said Amy.

'Why is it smiling?' asked Clarice suspiciously.

'I expect it wants to eat Beryl. Don't stare at it.'

She closed her eyes. When she was very small she had believed that not being able to see any-

106

thing also made her invisible.

The mongrel, fascinated by Mrs Pickett's wedding hat, stood on his hind legs for a closer look.

Then Beryl woke up.

She shrieked.

Everybody on the bus jumped with fright.

The dog fell backwards off the seat. The reader dropped his paper. The snoozer choked on a snore.

And Beryl just went on screaming.

The conductor and the old woman banged their heads together when they both bent down to grab the little dog.

'Shut up,' yelled Amy.

Beryl's hysterics ended as abruptly as they had begun.

Beryl

'I've had a nasty fright,' she snivelled and then made things much worse by standing up.

A speckled brown egg wobbled for a moment in artificial fruit before rolling off the back of the hat.

The bus made an unscheduled stop.

'Off,' said the conductor. 'I'm reporting you to

the RSPCA.'

'We've paid to go to the crossroads,' Amy reminded him.

'You've not paid for livestock,' he said severely, 'and there's egg all over my seat.'

So Amy and Clarice stood at the roadside and watched the bus trundle away towards Murdoch.

'I've been bitten,' said Amy, scratching under her arm.

'Oh, terrific,' said Clarice. 'She gets me in trouble at school, I waste my pocket-money on fares, the bus company's going to sue us and now we're lost – but all *she's* worried about is an itch. Terrific!'

'We're not lost,' said Amy, sulking.

Clarice set off back towards the village.

'You and that half-baked hen can find your own stupid straw.'

She kept in the centre of the road where nothing with teeth or horns could lunge out of the hedge at her.

Amy scratched under her other arm. All around her the countryside was quite still and quiet. A lark began disturbing the peace, thought better of it after a few twitters and went home for lunch. Miles and miles away, a tractor engine droned.

'We're lost,' she said in Chicken, 'and it's all your fault. Two days without an egg and then you go and lay one on the bus.'

'Hah!' jeered shameless Beryl. 'Call yourself one of us. Get organized, Pickett! I can smell farm from here.'

Amy realized that she could smell it, too. Like drains, only healthier.

She found a break in the hedge and looked across the fields. Stuck out in the tail-end of nowhere and just visible above some trees, the corrugated-iron roof of Bootlace Farm glittered nastily in the sun.

'Come back,' she yelled after Clarice.

It sounded more like an order than a request, so Clarice ignored it. She marched on down the road, wondering how the RSPCA would punish someone who wore a live chicken as a bonnet.

A ringed snake, just a bit fatter and longer than her recorder, slithered out of the ditch a few yards ahead and set off in the same direction down the road. Clarice almost trod on it.

'A serpent!' she wailed. 'Huge fangs! Ugh!'

109

It was actually a very shy and harmless grass snake but to Clarice, who only felt *really* safe with buildings all around her, it looked as if it might have escaped from a zoo. She fled back to Amy and found her using a stick to get at an itch in the middle of her back.

'I can't stand much more of this,' said Clarice, breathing hard. 'Chickens, dogs, snakes and now your fleas. What next?'

To find out, she had to squeeze through the gap in the hedge and trail along behind Amy, across fields of lavender-blue flax. All the way she fussed about snakes and got nowhere, like a dog with a concrete bone.

'Why don't they make a noise? Then we'd know where they were and keep clear.'

'Snakes hiss,' said Amy, scratching and scratching.

'This one didn't,' said Clarice. 'Anyway, hissing isn't loud enough. Why can't they *chirp* or something? Why aren't they pink or yellow so we can see them better?'

They clambered over a stone wall and walked round a stone barn and there they were, right in the middle of the Dibble farmyard. There were pigs in pig-pens and free-range pigs and a huge mound of steaming pig manure.

'Pooh!' said Amy.

'Yuk,' said Clarice. 'No wonder Bossy wears wellies in the summer.'

 'I fancy a lettuce for my lunch,' said Beryl.

The village where Amy and Clarice lived had everything a village needs. It had a pub and a garage, two shops, the school, a church, a police-man, a doctor and a plumber. It did not need Bootlace Farm.

'Let's go,' said Amy. 'We're trespassing.'

 'Oh, get on with it,' said Beryl. 'There'll be dry straw in the barn.'

 'We can't just *take* it,' said Amy meekly.

All the fight had gone out of her, that was the long and short of it. She felt suddenly very odd, shivery but hot, and her eyes ached. Her feet seemed a long way from her head, as if the top half of her body was using the bottom half of someone else.

'I can hear a voice,' said Clarice.

'Like Joan of Arc,' suggested Amy, feeling peculiar enough herself for something mystical to happen.

'Like the weather forecast, actually.'

Farmer Dibble and his wife always had the radio switched on in their kitchen when they ate. They preferred not to talk at mealtimes. Talking stopped them from chewing and swallowing. They spent a lot of time chewing and swallowing.

Sometimes they sat facing the open door so that they could stare at the television in the next room while they demolished huge plates of steaming food.

On the whole, what the Dibbles enjoyed most was to stuff as much into themselves as they could manage without actually bursting at the seams. Having the radio and the TV switched on, and the sound turned up high, somehow created the right atmosphere for gluttony. And Mrs Dibble liked to chew in time to music.

Any interruption to this feeding ritual upset them both very much. Which was why, although they both heard Clarice knocking on the front door, they chose to ignore her. Farmer Dibble increased the volume of sound on the radio and sheep three fields away heard the news.

'Right,' said Clarice. 'That's it. We tried.'

She went back to the stone barn and Amy trailed after her through oily green puddles of liquid manure.

Clarice pushed open the barn doors. A slab of sunlight fell across the bales of straw stacked from wall to wall and right up to the roof.

'They're not going to miss a little bit of *that*,' she said. 'We'll just take some and get out of here before Bossy gets home from school.'

'Yes, sir,' said Amy, scowling.

She still liked to be in charge even if she did feel peculiar.

The remains of a lady scarecrow lay like an uncomfortable corpse behind one of the doors. Her stuffed arms and legs, poking out of a sacking frock, were yards away from her head. She looked the way Amy felt.

'You keep watch,' said Clarice, pulling away at the sacking until it came free in a cloud of dust. 'Give me a warning if anyone comes.'

'How?'

Clarice sighed. 'I don't know,' she said. 'Any sort of warning. Don't bother to find a blanket and send up smoke signals. Make a cuckoo call or something.'

'At this time of year?' said Amy, determined to be awkward. 'Anyway, I can't do cuckoo calls.'

'Well, cluck like a chicken, then,' said Clarice, losing patience. 'You're good at that.'

She turned her back and set about filling the sack with straw.

Amy went outside, holding her nose. The pig smell was really terrible. She lurked about a bit in front of the barn and developed a headache.

 'Okay,' she said to Beryl. 'You'll have to come down now.'

She was actually raising her arms to remove the hat when the Dibble radio went silent.

The sudden quiet unsettled the pigs. They wallowed around uneasily and grunted. Then Clarice reappeared from the barn, dragging the sack behind her.

'Stop larking about,' she said urgently. 'Come and help before somebody sees us.'

They were struggling to lift their booty when the front door of the farmhouse banged open.

'We're dead,' said Clarice, deciding that God

114

must have gone out for the day.

Farmer Dibble stood on the step. He still had a napkin tucked into his shirt.

'Oy!' he yelled.

'How refined,' murmured Beryl. 'He should be able to get his money back from the charm school.'

'Clear off, you! This is private property.'

Mrs Dibble appeared behind him, a large growling Alsatian at her heels.

'You clear off,' she shouted, 'or I'll set Boris on you. Upsetting the pigs with that 'at. They're up to no good, Daddy.'

Her red face was as homely as a mud fence. Her body had muscles enough for three weight-lifters. She looked just like Farmer Dibble in a skirt and jumper.

'I know you,' she bawled, pointing at Amy. 'I know 'er, Daddy. It's that Pickett brat what's always cheeking our Liz.'

'Mummy,' bellowed Farmer Dibble, 'they been stealing the straw. I'll skin 'em alive.'

He ripped the napkin from his throat and charged across the yard. Amy and Clarice aban-

doned the sack and ran but Daddy Dibble was surprisingly agile for a bus-shelter in breeches. With hands the size of turnips, he lunged at Amy.

'Gotcha!' he roared.

With a squawk to freeze the blood, Beryl launched herself at the giant's nose.

Farmer Dibble let go of Amy's arm and tipped backwards. He sat down with a squelch in manure, his boots splayed out in front of him. He had a very surprised look on his face.

'Mummy,' he whined, 'I been bitten by an 'at.'

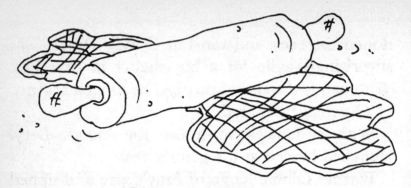

Chapter Eleven

Mrs Pickett arrived home at midday. As she fumbled for the front door key, she wondered if Keep Fit classes were really worth the bother. Her body ached, inside and out.

Every Monday morning she would set off to join her friends in the Village Hall, full of good intentions and imaginary sleeves rolled up for business. Two hours later, she would come trudging back home again, slumped over her bicycle and feeling as if she had one foot in the grave. All she wanted to do now was collapse onto a pile of cushions with a raspberry-ripple ice-cream.

As soon as she stepped into the house she knew that something was not quite right. Doors that she had closed were now ajar. A draught stirred her hair as if someone had left a window open. She found bits of cheese and breadcrumbs on the kitchen table. Drawers had been pulled out.

'Oh, help,' groaned Mrs Pickett, grabbing a rolling pin. 'Oh, sugar.'

She crept into the hall and listened without breathing before calling up the stairs.

'Trevor? Is that you?'

Silence filled the house. Somehow that was rather worse for Mrs Pickett than being suddenly confronted by A Criminal. Her insides turned to knitting.

'I'm a Black Belt,' she shouted bravely. 'Don't get me angry!'

She thought of running next door for Mrs Cooper and then remembered that Mrs Cooper would be working in Murdoch Library. For one moment she even thought of hiding in the cupboard under the stairs, until it occurred to her that The Criminal might be hiding there, too.

In the end, she did the sensible thing and telephoned the police.

Constable Wooders arrived ten minutes later, pudding-faced on a motorbike and looking sweaty in his leather gear. He was the sort of young man who always looked hot. Even in mid-winter, with snow a foot deep outside, if PC Wooders was in your house you felt you had to open a window for him.

He looked so huge and reassuring in the hallway that Mrs Pickett cheered up no end and wondered if she was making a lot of fuss about nothing. She forgot about the rolling pin and led him to the kichen. With a sweeping gesture, she indicated the breadcrumbs.

'Breadcrumbs,' said PC Wooders, trying some of them for taste.

'They weren't there when I went out,' said Mrs Pickett, feeling rather silly.

They went upstairs. PC Wooders was very thorough. He opened every cupboard and wardrobe. He pushed doors back so firmly that anyone hiding behind them would have been squashed flat. He rummaged under beds, with a great deal of creaking leather and grunting. He even looked under the bath and came out with a lot of fluff and a yellow plastic frog.

Mrs Pickett only found signs of a disturbance in her bedroom. PC Wooders was disappointed.

'Is that it, then? An empty box.'

He unzipped several pockets until he found his notebook. He would have preferred to unzip the leather jacket altogether, even to take it off, but that would have revealed to Mrs Pickett that he had nothing on underneath except a Mickey Mouse tattoo.

He sat down on the bed, licked the end of a pencil and made notes.

'Bread, butter, cheese,' he said.

'A nice bit of cheddar,' said Mrs Pickett, hoping that would make the theft of it sound more important. 'Trevor's favourite.'

'Hungry sneak thief,' said PC Wooders. 'Bound to be. Starving vagrant.'

Mrs Pickett said she thought that was doubtful. She found it hard to imagine her best hat on a tramp's head.

PC Wooders paused, the tip of the pencil on the tip of his tongue.

'Beg pardon?'

'I kept my hat in that,' said Mrs Pickett, pointing to the empty cardboard box.

PC Wooders sighed. He put away his notebook and stood up.

'Don't suppose your Amy's got anything to do with this?'

'Of course she hasn't,' said Mrs Pickett. 'She's at school.'

PC Wooders went to the window and looked down. There was a chicken sitting on the saddle of his motorbike.

'This hat,' he said, 'big straw contraption, is it? Lot of fruit and veg?'

'Something like,' said Mrs Pickett. 'Wore it at your wedding, Charlie.'

PC Wooders, who prided himself on his powers of observation but could not recall either the hat or Mrs Pickett at his wedding, blushed furiously.

'How many hens you got, Mrs P?'

'Only three,' said Mrs Pickett, expecting to be told she needed a government grant to keep them, 'besides Amy.'

'We've had a report in, see. About an hour ago. Kids causing a disturbance on a bus. One of them wearing a big hat with a fat old biddy roosting in it.'

'I told you,' said Mrs Pickett, her spirits beginning to flag again. 'She's at school.'

'All the same,' he said, 'why don't we go down now and count your chickens?'

When PC Wooders had gone away, roaring up the lane with his shiny leather bottom in the air,

Mrs Pickett lifted the telephone receiver. She dialled the number of All Saints School.

'Yes?' said Miss Metcalfe, after a good many brip-brips had echoed in Mrs Pickett's ear.

'I want to speak to my Amy, please.'

Miss Metcalfe made some gulping noises as she got her breath back. The school telephone was nowhere near the classroom and she had run all the way.

'So do I,' she said eventually.

'What?'

'Your Amy,' said Miss Metcalfe huffily, 'is not

here. Your Amy has not been here since ten o'clock this morning. She and Clarice Cooper have caused me no end of bother. What that Inspector's going to say in his report doesn't bear thinking of. I may have to leave the country. Right now, I'm hoping that's what your Amy's done.'

'Well, where is she?' asked Mrs Pickett, in a high state of indignation.

'How should I know?' Miss Metcalfe was sounding shrill as well. 'Why should I care? Not here, is where she is. Not in class where she should be. Your Amy's out there somewhere on the slippery slope to calamity, Mrs Pickett. Going downhill fast with the wind behind her!'

And she rang off.

Mrs Pickett went to the kitchen and made herself a pot of tea. Before she had even poured herself a second cup, things began to happen rather quickly.

First, the telephone rang but stopped ringing just as she reached it. (Miss Metcalfe, who had decided to say sorry for her fit of bad temper, had changed her mind. She would call on Mrs Pickett after school and apologize face to face.)

Then, while she was still standing in the hallway eyeing the receiver with extreme annoyance, Mrs

Pickett heard a commotion in the lane. This turned out to be Mr Pickett arriving home at exactly the same time as Mrs Cooper. As was usual when this happened there was a great deal of waving and tooting and shunting about until they managed to park.

And finally, siren blaring, a Murdoch police car drove up. Clarice was sitting in the front, giving the driver instructions. Amy lay flat out on the back seat with the wedding hat on her chest.

The terrible inhuman screeching, which sent Moses up a tree with his fur like a toothbrush, turned out not to be the car siren after all. It was fat Beryl shut in the boot.

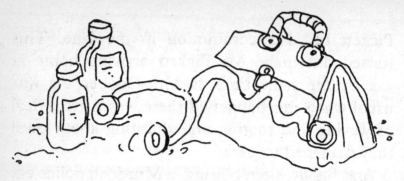

Chapter Twelve

Between them, the Picketts and Mrs Cooper soon polished off the little crowd that grew around the Murdoch police car. Then both families gathered in Mrs Pickett's kitchen to listen to Amy's explanation, with a few interruptions from Clarice and the Murdoch policeman. He was a cheerful chap, much older than PC Wooders, and had taken a shine to the two girls.

'First good laugh of the week,' he said. 'Kids will be kids.'

For once, Mrs Pickett was speechless. She sat at the kitchen table and stared at what remained of her wedding hat. It smelled so nasty she could not bring herself to touch it.

'Got three of me own,' said the policeman.

'Scamps, the lot of 'em. I like a kid with a bit of spirit.'

'I like them with a bit of common sense,' said Mrs Cooper and she took Clarice home for a bath.

Amy sat and scratched. The dizzy spells had passed but she still felt quite odd and swimmy. There had been a moment in the car when she thought she was going to be sick but the policeman gave her a peppermint and told her to lie flat.

'Did you know,' she said to her father, 'there are twice as many chickens as people? We could conquer the world.'

'Not another word,' shouted Mrs Pickett, feeling the strain. 'Go and have a bath. You're in a lot of trouble, young lady.'

'Don't she just pong something chronic,' said the cheerful policeman.

It seemed funny to be having a bath at half-past two in the afternoon but Amy went upstairs without a murmur. While the water ran, she undressed and pulled bits of straw from her wicked red hair.

'You'll have no trouble from that big bully Dibble,' said the Murdoch policeman, winking hugely as he got back into his car. 'I put it to him, quiet like. Bitten on the conk by an 'at! Never live it down, I says. Joke of the year. *He* won't be pressing no charges.'

Five minutes later, Mrs Pickett went upstairs and opened the bathroom door. She took one look at Amy splashing about and called for Mr Pickett to come and see. They stood in the steam together and stared at Amy's back. Mr Pickett went to the telephone.

'Hi!' said the Doctor. 'What's the prob?'

That was the way he spoke, like a television comedian. He was the sort of clown who called spectacles Face Furniture.

'It's our Amy,' said Mr Pickett.

'You should lock up those moth-balls.'

'It's not moth-balls this time, Doctor. It's chickens.'

'Chicken pox,' said the Doctor, misunderstanding. 'Okey-dokey. On my way.'

He examined Amy in the front room. First he tapped her on the chest. Then he listened to her breathing. He took her temperature. He even looked into her ears with a torch. Amy stuck out her tongue and said Aahh!

'What you have here, folks, is a very healthy

128

eight year old.'

'Who thinks she's a chicken,' said Mr Pickett.

'Say again.'

'She speaks to our hens,' said Mrs Pickett. 'She's forever clucking and laying eggs. Her teacher's fed up with it and so are we.'

'Is that all?' said the Doctor, pulling a funny face at Amy. 'I used to think I was a steam train. Hooted and chuffed for months. Drove everyone bananas.'

'She took one of our hens for an outing today. On a bus.'

'An outing, eh? Donkey rides? Bumper cars? Candy floss? Lovely grub!'

Mrs Pickett sighed, 'Turn round, Amy.' she said. 'Show Doctor your back.'

'Look at that, then,' said Mr Pickett. 'Only time I ever saw spots like them was on a potato.'

'Good grief,' said the Doctor. 'Blimey O'Riley!'

He took Amy closer to the window where the light was better.

'Is it a rash?' asked Mrs Pickett.

'Well, it's not designer stubble,' said the Doctor, touching Amy's skin.

'There's more under here,' she said, raising her arms. 'They itch a bit.'

'They would, love,' said the Doctor. 'You're growing feathers.'

'Feathers?' said Mrs Pickett faintly.

'I'll have to look it up, of course,' said the Doctor. 'This sort of thing isn't too common.'

'Where's she got *that* from, then?' asked Mr Pickett.

'Madam Marvel, of course,' said Amy, feeling better already.

The gossip about Amy spread quickly, as all choice tittle-tattle does in the countryside. Saying 'Can you keep a secret?' to someone who lives in a village is a bit like asking a starving man if he wants a piece of bread.

'She'll make a nice chicken,' said kind Melanie Watts. 'I think I'll knit her a nest.'

'I'll lay a trail of grub to the nearest microwave,' said Betty Dibble. 'She is DEAD MEAT!'

Little Pepe Jones, who had a nervous bladder, just wet himself with excitement.

'I'm really chuffed to bits,' said the Doctor, drinking champagne in Bedside Manor. 'If I was chocolate, I'd lick myself all over. Imagine! A patient turning into a chicken. This is going to make my name, you'll see. It'll be in all the medical journals. They'll be paying me to give lectures in America.'

'I could visit my Aunt Bella in New York,' said his wife, opening another bottle.

When Miss Metcalfe heard the news, she was not at all surprised.

'It explains quite a lot,' she said.

She had called round at what she hoped would be a quiet moment, to apologize for being rude on the telephone, only to find a crowd in the Pickett's front room: Mrs Cooper, the Vicar, PC Wooders and a reporter from the Murdoch Weekly Record.

'Everyone's going to stare at her and point,' said Mrs Pickett.

'Don't be silly, Lucille,' said Mrs Cooper. 'Black families aren't two a penny round here, you know. Everyone stared and pointed at *us* when we first came. They don't stare now. They've got used to us and they'll get used to Amy, too.'

'How's she ever going to be a hairdresser if she's a chicken? I've got a word or two to say to that Madam Marvel.'

'Madam Marvel?' said the reporter.

'My wife's good with a needle,' said PC Wooders, 'when you come to alter your Amy's clothes.'

'Think positive, dear,' said Mrs Cooper. 'You won't need to buy any more shoes. And no more dental appointments.'

'She could always get a job at Disney Land,' said Mr Pickett.

'God created every living creature,' said the Vicar, rehearsing his sermon for Sunday. 'Even little girls who eat moth-balls and turn into chickens. Nature must have her way.'

'Moth-balls?' said the reporter.

Miss Metcalfe thought: *I won't be going to church this Sunday. Sorry God.*

'I expect your Amy will be moving to the caravan now,' said PC Wooders.

'Not before Trevor's mended the roof,' said Mrs Pickett.

'Caravan?' said the reporter.

'She'll need a good run,' said Miss Metcalfe.

'She gets quite enough exercise already,' said Mrs Pickett.

'A *chicken*-run, I meant.'

'How do I make a chicken-run,' asked Mr Pickett.

'Chase it with a carving knife,' yelled PC Wooders, slapping his leather thigh.

Nobody else laughed so he tried again.

'Do you realize,' he said, winking at the Vicar, 'if you crossed a chicken with an octopus, everyone here could have a leg for tea?'

'Pardon me,' said the reporter, 'but where *is* the little girl?'

Amy and Clarice sat together in the doorway of the caravan, their legs swinging.

'What do I look like now?' asked Amy.

'An alien,' said Clarice. 'What do you *feel* like?'

'Plump and tender,' said Amy. 'Oven-ready.'

'You're daft as a brush, you are,' said Clarice. 'I'm off for my tea.'

Amy hardly noticed she had gone.

A strange shimmering dust danced in the air around the caravan. It made her eyes water and her scalp tingle. Her ears buzzed in her head. When she tried to tell the chickens what was happening, all that came out was a blood-curdling screech.

 'Oh shut up,' said Beryl. 'Don't *you* start.'

133

'You can hardly blame her,' said Maureen. 'Fancy laying an egg on a bus. How *could* you?'

 'I said I was sorry, didn't I?'

 'No eggs is what you said,' said Doreen. 'Broody old boiler.'

 'It really was too frightful of you, dear. So uncouth.'

 'You lot could win medals for Synchronized Nagging,' said Beryl. 'It was an accident, I tell you. I had a bad scare.'

The shimmering dust settled like Christmas-tree glitter all around Amy. Her shoes fell off. She stared at her feet. They were changing shape as she watched, growing smaller and smaller. As she reached down to touch them, her elbows began to flap and then folded themselves away into wings of sleek red feathers.

An odd clicking sensation made the middle of her face twitch. One moment she was chewing her lower lip and the next moment there was no lip

to chew. No teeth, either. If she squinted a bit, she could see her nose turning yellow and pointy.

A beak!

Like a good deed in a wicked world, she had finally turned into a chicken.

Clarice had got as far as the Pickett yard when the kitchen door suddenly opened and a crowd of people came out of the house.

'Everybody over there,' said the reporter from the Murdoch Weekly Record, focussing his camera on the dirty van. 'I want a shot of where it says *T. Pickett, Plumber.*'

'Say "Cheese",' said PC Wooders.

'Come and have your picture taken,' called Mrs Cooper but Clarice made a U-turn and went back to the caravan.

The three chickens stood around Amy's clothes, which lay in a heap on the floor. A fourth chicken shook itself free of Amy's jeans.

'Wow,' said Clarice, 'that was quick! You didn't even have claws a moment ago.'

'I don't half feel little,' said Amy.

But all Clarice heard was clucking.

She cleaned her spectacles and crouched down for a closer look.

Amy tried pecking at a little bug which was running a marathon across the floor. She missed it every time. It escaped into an apple.

'How about an egg for my tea?' said Clarice.

'Waarrk, Quaarrk,' said Amy.

136